3-

SPEECH FOR PSYCHE IN THE GOLDEN BOOK OF APULEIUS

All night, and as the wind lieth among
The cypress trees, he lay,
Nor held me save as air that brusheth by one
Close, and as the petals of flowers in falling
Waver and seem not drawn to earth, so he
Seemed over me to hover light as leaves
And closer me than air,
And music flowing through me seemed to open
Mine eyes upon new colours.
O winds, what wind can match the weight of him!

EZRA POUND

Psyche

LOUIS COUPERUS

Psyche

LUCIUS APULEIUS

Cupid and Psyche

Psyche translated from the Dutch by
B.S. Berrington
Cupid and Psyche translated by
Robert Graves

PUSHKIN PRESS
LONDON

Psyche first published in Dutch in 1898

Cupid and Psyche, from *The Golden Ass* by Lucius Apuleius,
translated by Robert Graves 1950, with the translation
subsequently edited by Michael Grant. Translation published
with permission of Carcanet Press.

Quotation on page 4, from *Collected Short Poems* by Ezra Pound,
1968, reproduced by permission of Faber and Faber Ltd.

This edition first published in 1999 by
Pushkin Press
22 Park Walk
London SW10 0AQ

British Library Cataloguing in Publication Data:
A catalogue record for this book is available
from the British Library

ISBN 1 901285 21 9

Set in $10^{1}/_{2}$ on $13^{1}/_{2}$ Baskerville
and printed in France by Expressions, Paris
on Rives Classic Laid

Cover illustration: *Bondi*
Jason Martin

I

GIGANTICALLY MASSIVE, with three hundred towers, on the summit of a rocky mountain, rose the king's castle high into the clouds.

But the summit was broad, and flat as a plateau, and the castle spread far out, for miles and miles, with ramparts and walls and pinnacles.

And everywhere rose up the towers, lost in the clouds, and the castle was like a city, built upon a lofty rock of basalt. Round the castle and far away lay the valleys of the kingdom, receding into the horizon, one after the other, and ever and ever.

Ever changing was the horizon: now pink, then silver; now blue, then golden; now grey, then white and misty, and gradually fading away. In clear weather there loomed behind the horizon always another horizon. They circled one another endlessly; they were lost in the dissolving mists, and suddenly their silhouette became more sharply defined.

An expanse of variegated clouds stretched away at times over the lofty towers, but below rushed a torrent, which fell like a cataract into a fathomless abyss, that made one dizzy to look at.

So it seemed as if the castle rose up to the highest stars and went down to the central nave of the earth.

Along the battlements, higher than a man, Psyche often wandered, wandered round the castle from tower to tower, from wall to wall, with a dreamy smile on her face, then she looked up and stretched out her hands to the stars, or gazed below at the dashing water, with all the colours of the rainbow, till her head grew dizzy, and she drew back and placed her little hands before her eyes. And long she would sit in the corner of an embrasure, her eyes looking far away, a smile on her face, her knees drawn up and her arms entwining them, and her tiny wings spread out against the mossy stone-work, like a butterfly that sat motionless.

And she gazed at the horizon, and however much she gazed, she always saw more.

Close by were the green valleys, dotted with grazing sheep, soft meadows with fat cattle, waving acorn-fields, canals covered with ships, and the cottage roofs of a village. Farther away were lines of woods, hill-tops, mountain-ridges, or a mass of angular, rough-hewn basalt.

Still farther off, misty towers with minarets and domes, cupolas and spires, smoking chimneys, and the outline of a broad river. Beyond, the horizon became milk-white, or like an opal, but not a line more was there, only tint, the reflection of the last glow of the sun, as if lakes were mirrored there; islands rose, low, in the air, aerial paradises, watery streaks of blue sea, oceans of ether and light quivering nothingness!...

And Psyche gazed and mused.... She was the third princess, the youngest daughter of the old king, monarch of the Kingdom of the Past.... She was always very lonely. Her sisters seldom saw her, her father only for a moment in the evening, before she went to bed; and when she had the chance she fled from the mumbling old nurse, and wandered along the battlements and dreamed, with her eyes far away, gazing at the vast kingdom, beyond which was nothingness....

Oh, how she longed to go farther than the castle, to the meadows, the woods, the towns—to go to the shining lakes, the opal islands, the oceans of ether, and then to that far, far-off nothingness, that quivered so, like a pale, pale light!... Would she ever be able to pass out of the gates?—Oh, how she longed to wander, to seek, to fly!... To fly, oh! To fly, to fly as the sparrows, the doves, the eagles!

And she flapped her weak, little wings.

On her tender shoulders there were two wings, like those of a very large butterfly, transparent membranes, covered with crimson and soft, yellow dust, streaked with azure and pink, where they were joined to her back. And on each wing glowed two eyes, like those on a peacock's tail, but more beautiful in colour and glistening like jewels, fine sapphires and emeralds on velvet, and the velvet eye set four times in the glittering texture of the wings.

Her wings she flapped, but with them she could not fly.

That, that was her great grief—that, that made her think, what were they for, those wings on her shoulders? And she shook them and flapped them but could not rise above the ground; her delicate form did not ascend into the air, her naked foot remained firm on the ground, and only her thin, fine veil, that trailed a little round her snow-white limbs, was slightly raised by the gentle fluttering of her wings.

II

TO FLY! OH, TO FLY!
She was so fond of birds. How she envied them! She enticed them with crumbs of bread, with grains of corn, and once she had rescued a dove from an eagle. The dove she had hidden under her veil, pressed close to her bosom, and the eagle she had courageously driven off with her hand, when in his flight he overshadowed her with his broad wings, calling out to him to go away and leave her dove unhurt.

Oh, to seek! To seek!

For she was so fond of flowers, and gladly in the woods and meadows, or farther away still, would she have sought for those that were unknown. But she cultivated them within the walls, on the rocky ground, and she had made herself a garden; the buds opened when she looked at them, the stems grew when she stroked them, and when she kissed a faded flower it became as fresh again as ever.

To wander, oh, to wander!

Then she wandered along the battlements, down the steps, over the courtyards and the ramparts, but at the gates stood the guards, rough and bearded and clad in mail, with loud-sounding horns round their shoulders.

Then she could go no farther and wandered back into the vaults and crypts, where sacred spiders wove their webs; and then, if she became frightened, she hurried away, farther, farther, farther, along endless galleries, between rows of motionless knights in armour, till she came again to her nurse, who sat ever at her spinning-wheel.

Oh! To glide through the air!

To glide in a steady wind, to the farthest horizon, to the milk-white and opal region, which she saw in her dreams, to the uttermost parts of the earth!

To glide to the seas, and the islands, which yonder, so far, far away and so unsubstantial, changed every moment, as if a breeze could alter their form, their tint; so unfirm, that no foot could tread them, but only a winged being like herself, a bird, a fairy, could gently hover over them, to see all that beautiful landscape, to enjoy that atmosphere, that dream of Paradise....

Oh! To fly, to seek, to wander, to soar!...

And for hours together she sat dreaming in an embrasure, and her wings spread out, like a little butterfly that sat motionless.

III

EMERALDA, that was the name of the eldest sister. Surpassingly beautiful was Emeralda, dazzling fair as no woman in the kingdom, no princess in other kingdoms. Exceedingly tall she was, and majestic in stature; erect she walked, stately and proudly; she was very proud, for after the death of the king she was to reign on the throne of the Kingdom of the Past. Jealous of all the power which would be hers, she rejected all the princes who sued for her hand. She never spoke but to command, and only to her father did she bow. She always wore heavy brocade, silver or gold, studded with jewels. And long mantles of rustling silk, fringed with broad ermine; a diadem of the finest jewels always glittered on her red golden hair and her eyes also were jewels, two magnificent green emeralds, in which a black carbuncle was the pupil; and people whispered secretly that her heart was cut out of one single, gigantic ruby.

Oh, Psyche was so afraid of her!

When Psyche wandered through the castle and suddenly saw Emeralda coming, preceded by pages, torches, shield-bearers, and maids-in-waiting, who bore her train, and a score of halberdiers, then she was struck with fear, and hastily concealed herself behind a door, a curtain, no matter where, and then Emeralda rustled by with a great noise of satin and gold and all the trampling of her retinue, and Psyche's heart beat loudly like a clock: tick! tick! tick! tick! till she thought she would faint....

Then she shut her eyes so as not to see the cold, proud look of Emeralda's green emeralds, which pierced through the curtains, and saw Psyche well enough, though she pretended not to see her. And when Emeralda was gone, then Psyche fled upstairs, high up on to the battlements, fetched a deep breath, pressed her hands to her bosom, and long afterwards her little wings trembled from fear. Astra, that was the name of the second princess. She wore a living star upon her head; she was very wise and learned; she knew much more than all the philosophers and learned men in the kingdom, who came to her for counsel.

She lived in the highest tower of the castle, and sometimes, along the bars of her window, she saw clouds pass by, like spirits of the mist. She never left the tower. She sat, surrounded by rolls of parchment, gigantic globes, which she turned with a pressure of her finger; and after hours of contemplation she described, with great compasses, on a slab of black marble, circle after circle, or reckoned out long sums, with numbers so great that no one could pronounce them.

Sometimes she sat surrounded by the sages of the land, and the king himself came and listened to his daughter, as in a low, firm voice she explained things. But because she possessed all the wisdom of the earth, she despised all the world, and she had had constructed on the terrace of her tower a telescope, miles long, through which she could look to every part of the illimitable firmament. And when the sages were gone, and she was alone, then she went on to the terrace and peered through the giant telescope, which she turned to all the points of the compass. Through the diamond lenses, cut without facets, she saw new stars, unknown to men, and gave them names. Through the diamond lenses she saw sun systems, spirals of fire, shrivel up through the illimitableness of the universe. . . . But she kept gazing, for behind those sun systems, she knew, were other spheres, other heavens, and there farther still, illimitably far, was the Mystic Rose, which she could never see. . . .

Sometimes, when Psyche wandered round the castle, she knocked nervously, inquisitively at Astra's door, who graciously allowed her to enter. When Astra stood before the board and reckoned out long sums, Psyche looked very earnestly at her sister's star, which glistened on her head, in her coal-black hair. Or she went on to the terrace and peeped through the telescope, but she saw nothing but very bright light, which made her eyes ache. . . .

IV

IN THE EVENING, before she went to sleep, Psyche sought the king.

A good hundred years old he was, his beard hung down to his girdle, and generally he sat reading the historical scrolls of the kingdom, which his ministers brought him every day.

But in the evening Psyche climbed on to his knees and nestled in his beard, or sat at his feet in the folds of his tabard, and the scroll fell to the ground, and crumpled up, and the withered hand of the mighty monarch stroked the head of his third child, the princess with the little wings.

"Father, dear," asked Psyche once; "why have I wings, and cannot fly?"

"You need not fly, child; you are much safer with me than if you were a little bird in the air."

"But why then have I wings?"

"I don't quite know, my child. . . ."

"Why have I wings, and Astra a living star upon her head, and Emeralda eyes of jewels?"

"Because you are princesses; they are different from other girls."

"And why, dear father," whispered Psyche, secretly, "has Emeralda a heart of ruby?..."

"No child, that she has not. She has, it is true, eyes of emerald, because she is a princess—as Astra has a star and you two pretty wings—but she has a human heart."

"No, father, dear, she has a heart of stone."

"But who says so, my child?"

"The nurse does, father, her own pages, the guards at the gates, and the wise men who come to Astra."

The king was very sad. He and his daughter looked deep into each other's eyes, and embraced each other, for the king was sad, because of what he saw in the future, and Psyche was frightened: she always trembled when she thought of Emeralda.

"Little Psyche," said her old father, "will you now promise me something?"

"Yes, father, dear."

"Will you always stay with me, little Psyche? You are safe here, are you not? And the world is so great, the world is so wicked. The world is full of temptation and mystery. Winged horses soar through the air; gigantic sphinxes lurk in the deserts; devilish fauns roam through the forests.... In the world, tears are shed, which form brooks, and in the world people give away their noblest right for the lowest pleasure.... Stay with me, Psyche, never wander too far away, for under our castle glows the Netherworld!... And life is like a princess, a cruel princess with a heart of stone...."

Of precious stone, like Emeralda, thought Psyche to herself. Who rides in triumph with her victorious chariot over the tenderest and dearest, and presses them stone-dead into the deepest furrows of the earth....

"Oh, Psyche, little Psyche, promise me always to stay here in this high and safe castle; always to stay with your father!"

She did not understand him.

His eyes, very large and animated, looked over her into space, with inexpressible sadness. Then she longed to console him, and threw her white arms around his neck; she hid herself, as it were, in his beard, and she whispered playfully:

"I will always stay with you, father dear...."

Then he pressed her to his heart, and thought that he would soon die....

V

PSYCHE WAS OFTEN very lonely, but yet she had much: she had the flowers, the birds; she had the butterflies, which thought that she was a bigger sister; she had the lizards, with which she played, and which, like little emeralds, she held against her veil; she had the swans in the deep castle moats, which followed when she walked on the ramparts; she had the clouds, which came floating from distant islands and paradises beyond; she had the wind, which sang her ballads; the rain, which fell down wet upon her and covered her wings with pearls. She would gladly have played with the pages in the halls, have laughed with the shield-bearers in the armoury, have listened to the martial tales of the bearded halberdiers at the gates, but she was a princess and knew she could not do that, and she always walked past them with great dignity, maidenly modest in her fine, thin veil, which left her tender limbs half exposed. That was the noble Nakedness, which was her privilege as a princess, a privilege given her at her cradle, together with her wings by the Fairy of Births, as to Emeralda was given the Jewel and to Astra the star. For never might Psyche

wear Jewel or Star, and never might Emeralda or
Astra go naked. Each princess had her own privilege,
her birthright. Adorable was Psyche as, unconscious of
her maidenly tender purity, she was seen with her
crimson glittering wings, naked in the folds of her veil,
walking past the armour-bearers and soldiers, who
presented their swords or halberds as the princess,
nymph-white, stepped past them.

Psyche was often very lonely, for her nurse was old and
mumbled over her spinning-wheel; playmates Psyche
had not, because she was a princess, and she would not
get court-ladies till she was older and more dignified. But
with the birds and the clouds and the wind Psyche could
speak and laugh, and she was seldom dull, although she
sometimes wished she were no longer *Princess of Nakedness*
with the wings, but one of those very ordinary peasant-
girls whom she had seen milking the cows, or plucking
the thick bunches of grapes in the vineyard at harvest-
time, whilst the grape-pressers, handsome brown lads
with sturdy arms, encircled the girls and danced.

But Psyche wandered along the ramparts; she
looked at the clouds and spoke with the wind, and she
asked the wind to give flight to her wings, so that she
could fly far off to the opal landscapes that kept shift-
ing and changing. But the wind rushed away with a
flapping noise of wings that Psyche envied, and her
own wings flapped a little, but in vain.

Psyche looked at the clouds. They floated along so stately in all kinds of forms—in the forms of sheep, swans, horses—and the form never remained: the seeming forms, thick-white in the blue ether, were constantly changing. Now she saw three swans which were drawing a boat, in which stood three women, who guided the swans; then she saw the women become a tower, the swans a dragon, and from far, far away came a knight, sitting on a winged horse. But now slowly the scene changed into a flock of little silver-fleeced, downy sheep, which were browsing far off in the sunshine as in a golden meadow. The knight disappeared, but the horse glided nearer and flew on his wings, high over the castle, towards the sheep.

Then Psyche dreamed at night of the swans, the tower, the dragon, the knight, the horse; but the horse she liked best, because it had strong wings. And next morning she gazed from the battlements to see if the horse would come again.

But then the sky was either gloomy from the rain or blue from the absence of clouds, or covered with white peacock's feathers, splendid plumes, but motionless, far, far away in the air. The wind changed, when she said: "Away! blow now from the East again! Begone, North wind, with your dark perils, begone! Begone, West wind, with your rain-urns! Begone, South wind, with your peacock's feathers! Come now, wind from the East, with

your treasures of luxurious visions, ye dragons, ye horses, ye girls with swans!..." Then the clouds began to
shift, the winds to blow, and play an opera high up in the
air, and Psyche, enchanted, sat and gazed.

Then after weeks, after she had missed it for weeks,
came again the winged horse.

And she beckoned to it to approach, to descend to
her; but it flew past over the castle. Then she missed it
again for many days, and, angry, she looked at the sky
and scolded the wind. But then the horse came again,
and, laughing, she beckoned to it. The horse ascended
high, its wings expanded in the air, and oh, wonder! it
beckoned to her to come up, up to it. She gave a sign
that she could not, shook her little shoulders helpless-
ly, and, trembling, flapped her wings and spread her
arms wide out to say that she could not. And the horse
sped away on the breath of the wind from the East.

Then Psyche wept, and, sad at heart, sat looking at
the far, far-off landscapes which she would never reach.

But weeks afterwards the treasure-bringing wind
blew again, and again appeared the horse in the horizon, and it flew near and beckoned to Psyche, her
heart heavy with hope and fear.... The horse mounted up; it beckoned to her.... She gave a sign that she
could not; and oh! she feared that it would speed away
again, the horse with the strong wings.

No ... no ... the horse descended!

Then Psyche uttered a joyful cry, sprang up, danced with delight and clapped her little hands. From the lofty, lofty sky the horse came down, gliding on his broad wings. It came down.

And Psyche, the little, joyful, excited Psyche, saw it coming, coming down to her. It descended —it approached. Oh, what a beautiful horse it was! Greater than the greatest horses, and then with wings! Fair it was, fair as the sun, with a long curly mane and long flowing tail, like a streamer of sunny gold. The noble head on its arched neck proudly raised and its eyes shone like fire, and a stream of breath came from its expanded nostrils, cloud after cloud. Big, powerful, muscular, its wings were stretched out like silvery quills, as Psyche had never seen in a bird. And its golden hoofs struck the clouds and made them thunder; and sparks of fire shot forth in the pure, clear daylight. Enraptured Psyche had never seen such a beautiful horse before, never a bird so beautiful; and breathless, with her head raised, she waited till it should descend, descend on the terrace. . . . At last there it stood before her. Its nostrils steamed, and its hoofs struck sparks from the basalt rock, and it waved its mane and swished its tail.

"Splendid, beautiful horse," said Psyche, "who are you?"

"I am the *Chimera*," answered the horse, and his voice sounded deep as the clang of a brazen clock.

"Can you really speak?" asked Psyche, astonished. "And fly? Oh, how happy you must be!"

"Why have you called me, little princess?" said the Chimera.

"I wanted to see you quite near," replied Psyche. "I only saw you dart like winged lightning through the air, so soon were you away again; and I was always sorry when I could not see you any more. Then I became, oh, so sad!"

"And why did you want to see me quite near, little princess with the wings?"

"I find you so beautiful. I have never seen anything so beautiful; I did not know that anything so beautiful existed. What are you? A horse you are not. Nor a dragon either, nor a man. What are you?"

"I am the Chimera."

"Where do you come from?"

"From far away. From the lands which are beyond the lands, from the worlds beyond the worlds, from the heavens beyond the heavens."

"Where are you going?"

"Very far. Do you see those distant regions yonder, of silver and opal? Well, thousands of times so far I am going .... I go from illimitableness to illimitableness; I come from nothingness and I am going to nothingness."

"What is nothingness?"

"Everything. Nothingness is as far as your brain can think, my little princess; and then still farther, and nothingness is more than all that you see from this high tower...."

"Are you never tired?"

"No, my wings are strong; I can bear all mankind on my back, and I could carry them away to the stars behind the stars."

"If Astra knew that!"

"Astra knows it. But she does not want me. She reckons out the stars with figures."

"Why do you fly from one end to the other, O splendid Chimera? What is your object? What are you for?"

"What is your own object, little Psyche? What are you yourself for? For what are flowers, men, the stars? Who knows?"

"Astra...."

"No, Astra knows nothing. Her knowledge is founded on a fundamental error. All her knowledge is like a tower, which will fall down."

"I should like to know much. I should like to know more. I should like to seek far through the universe. I long for what is most beautiful.... But I do not know what it is. Perhaps you yourself are what is most beautiful, Chimera.... But why are you now spreading out your wings?"

"I must go."

PSYCHE

"So soon? Whence? Oh, why are you going so soon, splendid Chimera?"

"I must. I must traverse illimitableness. I have already stayed here too long."

"Stay a little longer...."

"I cannot. I may not."

"Who compels you, O powerful horse, quick as lightning?..."

"Power."

"What is power?"

"God...."

"Who is God? Oh, tell me more! Tell me more! Don't go away yet! I want to ask you so much, to hear so much. I am so stupid. I have longed so for you. Now you have come, and now you want to go away again."

"Do not ask me for wisdom; I have none. Ask the Sphinx for wisdom, ask me for flight."

"Oh, stay a little longer! Don't flap so with your flaming wings! Who is the Sphinx? O Chimera, do not give me wisdom, but flight!"

"Not now...."

"When, then?"

"Later...."

"When is that?"

"Farewell."

"O Chimera, Chimera!..."

The horse had already spread out his wings broad.

32

He was ascending. But Psyche suddenly threw both her arms round his neck and hung on to his mane.

"Let me go, little princess!" cried the horse. "I ascend quickly, and you will fall, to be dashed to pieces on the rock! Loose me!"

And slowly he ascended....

Psyche was afraid; she let go her arms; she became dizzy, fell against the pinnacle, and bruised one of her wings. That pained her ... but she heeded it not; the horse was already high in the air, and she followed his track with her eyes....

"He is gone," thought she. "Will he come again? Or have I seen him for the first and last time?"

"As a dream he came from far-off regions, and to still farther regions he has gone.... Oh, how dull the world seems! How dead is the horizon! And how dizzy I feel.... My wing pains me...."

With her hand she smoothed the wrinkle out of her wing; she stroked it till it was smooth again, and tears ran down her cheeks.

"Horrid wings! They cannot fly, they cannot follow the strong Chimera! I'm in such trouble, such trouble!! But ... no.... Is that trouble? Is that happiness? I know not ... I am very happy!... I am so sorrowful.... How beautiful he was! how strong, how sleek, how splendid, how quick, how wise, how noble, how broad his wings! How broad his wings! How weak I am compared to him. . . . A child, a weak child; a weak, naked child with little wings. . . . O Chimera, my Chimera, O Chimera of my desire, come back! Come back!! Come back!! I cannot live without you; and if you do not come again, Chimera, then I will not live any longer lonely in this high castle. I will throw myself into the cataract. . . ."

She stood up, her eyes looking eagerly into the empty air. She pressed her hands to her bosom, she wept, and her wings trembled as if from fever.

Then suddenly, she saw the king, her father, sitting at the bow-window of his room. He did not see her, he was reading a scroll. But anxious lest he should see her trouble, her despair, and longing desire, she fled, along the battlements, the ramparts, through the passages and halls of the castle, till she came to the tower, where her nurse sat at her spinning-wheel, and then she fell down at the feet of the old woman and sobbed aloud.

"What is it, darling?" asked the old crone, frightened. "Princess, what is it?"

"I have hurt my wing!" sobbed Psyche.

And she showed the nurse the wrinkle in her wing, which was not yet quite gone.

Then, with soothing voice and wrinkled hand, the old nurse slowly stroked the painful wing till it became smooth.

VI

THE OLD KING, assisted by pages, sat down slowly on his throne; his ministers and courtiers gathered round him. Then there was a great rustling of satin and gold, and in came Emeralda, the Princess Royal, the Princess of the Jewel, as her title ran: first pages, life-guards, and then she herself, glittering with splendour, in her dress of silver-coloured silk; her bosom blazed with emeralds, a tiara of emeralds adorned her temples; her red-golden tresses, intertwined with emeralds, fell in three-fold plaits down each side of her face, from which the eyes of emerald looked proud, soulless, ice-cold, and arrogant. Court-ladies bore her train. A great retinue of halberdiers surrounded her jewelled majesty, and as she passed along, the trembling courtiers bowed lower to her than they did to the king, because they were in deadly fear of her.

Astra, with dragging step, followed her. She wore a dress of azure covered with stars, a white mantle full of stars, and her living star sparkled in her coal-black hair.

The sages of the country surrounded her: grey-haired men in velvet tabards, with very long silver beards, dim eyes, and wise, close-pressed lips.

The two princesses sat down on either side of the throne.

And for a moment the middle space of the hall between the waiting crowd remained empty. But then appeared Psyche, the third daughter, the Princess of Nakedness with the wings! Shyly she approached, looking right and left, with the laugh of a child. She was naked: only a golden veil was tied in a fold round her hips. Her wings were spread out like a butterfly's. She had no retinue: only her old nurse followed her; and she was so pretty and charming that people forgot to bow as she passed along, that the courtiers smiled and whispered, full of admiration, because she was so beautiful in her pure chastity. Slowly she walked along, shy and laughing a little; then close to the throne, where her father saw her approaching hesitatingly, her bare foot got entangled in her trailing golden veil, and to ascend the steps she lifted it up, knelt down, and kissed the king's hand.

Then calmly she sat down on a cushion at his feet, and was no longer shy. She looked round inquisitively and nodded a greeting here and there, child as she was, till all at once, to the right of the throne, she met the emerald look of Emeralda, and started and shivered; a cold thrill shot through her limbs, and she hid herself in the ermine of her father's mantle to be safe and warm.

Then there was a flourish of trumpets, and at the door of the Hall heralds announced Prince Eros, the youthful monarch of the Kingdom of the Present. He came in all alone. He was as beautiful as a god, with light-brown hair and light-brown eyes. He wore a white suit of armour over a silver shirt of mail, and his whole presence portrayed simplicity and intelligence.

The courtiers were astonished at his coming without a suite; Emeralda laughed scornfully aside with one of her court-ladies. She did not find him a king, that plain youth in his plain dress. But Eros had now approached and bowed low before the mighty monarch, and the latter bade him welcome with fatherly condescension.

Then spoke the prince:

"Mighty Majesty of the Past, accept my respectful thanks for your welcome. Diffident I come to your throne, for I am young in years, have little wisdom, little power. You reign over an extensive kingdom, the horizon of which is lost in illimitableness. I reign over a country that is not larger than a garden. From my humble palace, that is like a country-house, I can survey all my territory. Your Majesty, in spite of my poverty and insignificance, receives me with much honour and acknowledges me as sovereign in my kingdom; fills my heart with joy. Will your Majesty permit me to kneel and pay my homage to you as an obedient vassal?"

Then the old king nodded to Psyche, and the princess rose, because Eros was about to kneel.

Then said the king: "Amiable Eros, I love you as a son. Tell me, have you any wish that I can satisfy? If so, then it is granted you."

Then said Eros: "Your Majesty makes my heart rejoice by saying that you love me as a son. Well, then, my greatest joy would be to marry one of the noble princesses, who are your Majesty's daughters. But I am a poor prince, and whilst confessing to your Majesty my bold desire, I fear that you may think me too arrogant in presuming to cherish a wish that aims so high...."

"Noble prince," said the king, "you are poor, but of high birth and divine origin, higher and more divine than we. You are descended from the god Eros; we from his beloved Psyche. The history of the gods is to be read in the historical rolls of our kingdom. It would make my heart rejoice if you found a spouse in one of my princesses. But they are free in their choice, and you will have to win their love. Permit me, therefore, first of all to present to you my eldest daughter, the Princess Royal, Princess of the Jewel: Emeralda...."

Emeralda rose, and bowed with a scornful sneer.

"And," continued the monarch, "in the second place, to my wise Astra, Princess of the Star...."

Astra rose and bowed, her look far away, as if lost in contemplation.

"And would Emeralda permit me to sue for her love and her hand?" asked the prince.

"Majesty of the Present," replied Emeralda, "my father says that you are of more divine origin than we. I, your humble slave, consider it therefore too great an honour that you should be willing to raise me to your side upon your throne. And I accept your homage, but on one condition. that condition is: that you seek for me the All-Sacred Jewel, Jewel of Mystery, the name of which may not be uttered, the noble stone of Supremacy. The legends respecting this jewel are innumerable, inexplicable and contradictory. But the Jewel exists. Tell me, ye wise men of the land—tell me, Astra, my sister, does the Jewel exist?"

"It exists!" said Astra.

"It exists!" said all the wise men after her.

"It exists!" repeated Emeralda. "Prince, I dare ask much of you, but I ask you the greatest thing that our soul and ambition can think of. If you find me beautiful and love me, then seek, and bring me the Jewel, and I will be your wife, and together we shall be the most powerful monarchs in the world."

The prince bowed, and with imperceptible irony said:

"Royal Highness of the Jewel, your words breathe the splendour of yourself, and I will weigh them in my mind. Your beauty is dazzling, and to reign with you over the united kingdoms of the Past and the Present, appears to me indeed a divine happiness...."

"For other kingdoms exist not," added Astra, and the wise men repeated her words.

"Yes," murmured the king. "There is another kingdom...."

"What kingdom?" asked all.

"The kingdom of the Future," said the king, in a low tone.

Emeralda laughed scornfully. Astra looked compassionately. The wise men glanced at each other; the courtiers shook their heads.

"The king is getting old," they whispered. "The mind of His Majesty often wanders," muttered the ministers.

"Our monarch has always had much imagination," said the wise men. "He is a poet...."

But then spoke the prince.

"And you, wise Astra, Royal Highness of the Star, will you, like Emeralda, allow me to sue for your hand and heart?"

"Most willingly, Prince Eros!" said Astra, with a far-off look and in a vague tone.

"But I have conditions to make as well as Emeralda, the Princess Royal. Will you hear them? Then listen. If you see any chance of lengthening my telescope, of strengthening the lenses, that I can see through them

40

to the confines of the universe, to the last sun-system, to the Mystic Rose, to the Godhead Himself, then I will be your wife, and together we shall be the most powerful beings of the world, because then we are omniscient. For the universe is limited...."

"The universe is limited!" said the wise men, after her.

"Endless is the universe!" said the king, in a subdued voice.

The people laughed and shook their heads.

"The king is getting very old," was repeated everywhere.

"The king will soon die," prophesied the wise men, in a low tone. "He speaks like an old man, without reason; he will soon die...."

"Royal Highness of the Star," said the prince, "your words, pregnant with wisdom, I will also consider. For to be omniscient must indeed be the greatest power. But your Majesty has a third princess," he continued, addressing the king. "Where is she?"

"She is here," said the king. "She is the Princess of Nakedness with the wings. But she is still a child, Prince...."

Psyche blushed and bowed.

The prince looked long at her. Then he said to her, gently: "Your Highness is called Psyche? You have the name of the ancestress of your race, as I have the name of the god who begot mine. Is it not true?"

"I believe so," murmured Psyche, embarrassed.

"She is still a child, prince—forgive her!" repeated the king.

"Will your Majesty not permit me to ask for the hand and heart of your third daughter, the princess?"

"Certainly, prince; but she is still so young. . . . If she leaves me I shall be very sad. But if she loves you, then I will give her up to you, for then she will be happy. . . ."

"Tell me, Psyche, will you be my wife?"

Psyche blushed exceedingly. Her naked limbs blushed, her wings blushed.

"Prince," said she hesitatingly and looked bashfully at her father, "you do me much honour. But my sisters are more beautiful and wiser than I. And my father would miss me if I went with you to the kingdom of the Present."

"But tell me, Psyche, what conditions do you impose upon me?"

Psyche hesitated. She was about to exclaim joyfully: "Catch me the Chimera, bind him in a meadow to graze, and give me power over him, that I may mount his back and fly through the air as I like."

But she dared not before the whole court and her father. And so she only stammered: "None, prince. . . ."

"Could you love me?"

"I don't know, prince...."

Psyche was shy. She kept blushing, and all at once began to tremble and weep.

And she looked round to the king, fled to his arms, hid her face in his beard and sobbed.

"Prince Eros," said the king, "forgive her. You see she is a child. Seek for Emeralda's Jewel, or seek for Astra the Glass which will bring to view the confines of the universe; but leave me my youngest child."

Then the prince bowed. An indescribable sadness rose in his soul, like a sea. And pale he stammered, "I obey your Majesty."

Then the king descended from his throne and embraced the prince. And whilst the fanfares sounded, he put his arm through the arm of Eros, took Psyche by the hand, and conducted his guest to the banquet, the princesses following, surrounded by the whole court.

VII

FOR DAYS had Psyche watched in vain, and all hope died out of her heart.

But one windy morning—the thick white clouds were speeding through the air—she saw the desire of her heart again. Far away appeared a cloud, but as it drew nearer it became a horse: it was the Chimera.

She beckoned to it, and the Chimera came down.

"What do you want, little Psyche?"

She clasped her hands imploringly. "Take me with you...."

"You will become dizzy...."

"No, no...."

He descended, stamping on the basalt rock; the terrace shook, sparks flew up, and the steam of his breath shot out in clouds.

"Take me with you," she implored.

"Where do you wish to go?"

"To the islands of opal and silver."

"They are too far away."

"Take me, then, nearer to them; take me with you where you will."

"Are you not afraid?"

"No."

"Will you hold fast to my neck?"

"Yes, oh yes!"

"Come, then...."

She uttered a cry of joy. He bent his knees, and she got up with a beating, thumping heart. Between his flaming wings, on his broad, broad back, she sat almost as safe as in a nest of silver feathers.

"Trust not to my wings," he warned her; "I move them at every stroke. They open and shut, open and shut. Hold fast on to my neck. Clasp my mane. If you are not frightened and do not become giddy and sick, you will not fall, however high I go. "Do you dare, Psyche?"

"Yes."

She fastened his mane round her waist, as if it were strong rope of golden flax. She put her arms round his neck.

"I am ready," she said courageously.

He ascended, very slowly, with his broad wings. Under him, under her, the terrace sank away.

She shut her eyes, she held her breath, and the blood left her heart. Under her the castle sank away.

"Stop!" she implored. "I am dying...."

"I thought so, Psyche. You are much too weak. You cannot go up with me...."

She opened her eyes slightly. She sat on his back in

the silver down, where his quills clave to his light-gold loins. And round her, circles of light revolved, one after the other, and made her dizzy.

"Descend!" she implored. "Oh, descend! I cannot endure it. I have no breath; I am dying."

He descended.... He stood on the terrace. She slid along his wing to the ground. She put her hands before her face, and when she opened her eyes she was alone.

Then she was very, very sad. But next day, he appeared again. And, more courageous, she wished to mount him again. He let her do as she desired, and she got on his back. She shut her eyes, but smiled. He went higher and higher with her, without her saying "Descend." She travelled for a time high up in the air, she opened her eyes and kept smiling; she got accustomed to the rarefied air. The third time he soared away with her; she saw, far below, the royal castle, small as a toy, towers, ramparts; and then she realised for the first time that she had left the castle.

She thought of the king.

"Take me back!" she said to the horse commandingly.

He obeyed her. He took her back. But as soon as he was gone, she longed again for him and the lofty air. And she had but one thought, the Chimera. She no longer cared for the flowers which she had planted between the walls, and the flowers withered. She no longer cared for the swans, and the swans, neglected, followed her in vain, in the green moats; she forgot to crumble bread for them. And she looked at the clouds and she gazed at the wind, thinking only of him, the light-gold horse with the silver wings, because her came on the wind, on the clouds, which thundered when he struck with his hoofs.

On the day that he did not come, her fair Chimera, she sat pale and lonely, gazing from the battlements, her eyes far away, her arms round her knees. In the evening she nestled in the king's beard, in the folds of his tabard, but she dared not tell him that she had ridden a wondrous winged horse and flown with him through the air. But on the days that her beloved horse had come and taken her away with him, carefully flapping his wings, her face shone with golden happiness in the apotheosis of her soul, and through the gloomy halls, where sacred spiders, which were never disturbed, wove their webs, rang Psyche's high voice, and from the faded gobelin the low vault and the motionless iron knights strangely re-echoed the words of her joyous song.

VIII

"PSYCHE, where do you wish to go?"

"To the opal islands, to the seas of light, to the far-off luminous streaks. . . ."

"Take a deep breath; hold fast on to my neck; twist my mane more tightly round your hand, then we will begin our journey."

The clouds sent forth a rumbling sound of thunder; the Chimera's hoofs shot fire; his wings expanded and shut, and his strong feathers rustled in the air.

Psyche uttered a cry.

She had ascended higher than ever before, and under them sank away the castle, the meadows, the woods, the cities, and river; under them, like a map, lay stretched out province after province, desert after desert, the whole Kingdom of the Past. How great it was! How great it was! The frontiers receded from view again and again; far down below rose up town after town; river after river meandered along, mountain-ranges rose up one after the other, now only slightly elevated, then rising arabesquely through the plains. Then there were great waters like oceans, and Psyche saw nothing but white foaming sea. But on the other side of it began again the strand, the land, the wood, the meadows, the mountains, and so on endlessly....

"How much farther away are the opal islands, the streaks of light I see in the distance, my beloved Chimera?"

"We have passed them...."

She raised her head, bent over his streaming neck, and gazed about her.

"But I do not see them any longer!" she said, astonished. "I see wood and meadow, towns and mountains.... Is the world, then, the same everywhere? Where are the opal islands?"

"Behind us...."

"But I do not see them.... Have we passed them without my seeing them? O naughty Chimera, you did not tell me!"

"And where are the luminous streaks of the far-off land?"

"We are going through them...."

"I see nothing.... Below, land; around, clouds, as everywhere. But no lands of light.... And yet there, in the distance, very far away—what is that, Chimera? I see, as it were, a purple desert on a sea of golden water, with winding borders of soft mother-of-pearl; in the desert are oases like pale emerald, palms with silvery waving tops, azure bananas; and over the purple desert trills ether of light crimson, with streaks of topaz.... Chimera, Chimera, what is that country? What is that beautiful country? The golden sea with its foam forms a pearly fringe along the shore; the palms wave their tops to a rhythm of aerial music, and the bananas, blue, pink glow in the ether till all is light there!... Chimera, is that the rainbow?"

"No...."

"Chimera, is that the land of happiness? Is that the kingdom of happiness? Chimera, are you king there?"

"Yes, that is my country. And I am king there."

"Are we going thither?"

"Yes."

"Do you remain there, Chimera? Do we remain there together?"

"No...."

"Why not?"

"As soon as I have reached my purple land, I must go farther ... and then back again."

"O Chimera, I will not go back! I will forget everything—my father, my country. I will remain there with you!"

"I cannot.... But now pay great attention; we are approaching my kingdom, little Psyche. Look! Now we are going over the sea, now we are approaching the shore, lined with soft mother-of-pearl."

"The sea is a dirty green, like an ordinary sea; the borders are sand.... You are deceiving me, Chimera!

51

As soon as we approach, then you charm away every-thing that I saw beautiful."

"Now, under us is the purple desert; under us are the oases of pale emerald."

"You are deceiving me, Chimera! The desert glows in the strong sun, the oases fade away to nothing, like a meteor ... Chimera!"

"What, Psyche?"

"Where are you going?"

"To the land, as far off as you can see...."

"I care not about it! You always deceive me! You carry me away through endless space, and everything beautiful that I see disappears from my view. But yet ... there, behind the horizon, behind the sand of the desert, is a dazzling scene.... Are those silver grottos on a sea of light? Does the light there wave like water? Are those groves of light, cities of light, in a land of light? Tell me, Chimera, do people of light live there? Is that Paradise?"

"Yes, will you go thither?"

"Yes, oh yes, Chimera. There is happiness, the high-est happiness, and there I will remain with you!...

"We are now approaching it...."

"Let that land of light now stay, the paradise of glowing sunshine; do not charm away the land of hap-piness, O naughty Chimera: go to it now with me, and descend with me...."

"We are there...."

"Descend...."

He descended.

"Have we not yet reached the ground of light?"

"Look below: can you see nothing ?..."

She looked along his wing.

"I see nothing!... It is night.... It is dark....
Chimera!"

"What, little Psyche?"

"Where is the land of silver light, the land of the people of light. Where is it gone?"

"Do you not see it?"

"No...."

"Then it is gone...."

"Whither?"

"Behind us, under us...."

"Why did you not descend sooner?"

"My flight was too quick, and I could not,
Psyche...."

"You are deceiving me! You could have done so.
You would not.... Now ... now it is night, pitch dark,
starless night.... There is an icy coldness in the air....
O Chimera, take me back...."

He turned with a swing of his powerful wings. And
as he turned, the lightning broke forth and darted
zigzag through the air, like smooth-bright electric
swords; the black clouds parted asunder with a violent

peal of thunder like the clapping of cymbals, a storm of wind arose, the rain fell down in torrents....

"O Chimera, take me back!"

She threw herself on to his neck; she hid her face in his mane, and through the bursting storm, whilst at every blow of his hoofs it lightened round them, he winged his way, back with her to her country: the Kingdom of the Past, inky there, in the inky night....

IX

THE OLD KING WAS DEAD.

Black flags hung from the three hundred towers, and cast their dark shadows below.

A dim light fell, through the bow-windows into the castle, for the three hundred flags obscured the sun.

With funeral music, that made the heart feel sad, the procession, with long flickering torches, followed the king's coffin down the steps to the deep vaults below.

The priests, in black, prayed in Latin; the court, in black, sang the litany; and the princesses, in black, sang alternately a long Latin sentence....

Behind the coffin walked, first, Emeralda; behind her, Astra her sister; and then little Psyche, wrapped in her black veil. Emeralda sang with a voice of crystal; Astra, distracted, was too late in answering; and Psyche's voice trembled when she had to sing alone the long monotonous sentence....

There, in the deepest vault, they placed the coffin, next to the coffin of the king's father, and kneeling round it, they prayed. The low Roman vaults receded in impenetrable darkness. They sang and prayed the whole live-long day, and Psyche was very tired; and whilst she was kneeling, her little knees quite stiff, she fell asleep against the coffin of her late father. Her last thought had been to kiss the dear old face for the last time, but she felt nothing but the goldsmith's work, and the great round jewels that were in it hurt her head.... Then she fell asleep....

And when the court had prayed, and all went up the steps again, there above, to do homage to Emeralda, as queen of the Kingdom of the Past, they all forgot Psyche.

Long, long she slept....

And when she awoke, she did not know at first where she was.

Then by the light of the long torches she espied the coffin.

And through the crystal of the sarcophagus she saw the dead face of the king, and pressed a kiss upon the glass.

"Dear father!" she whispered, trembling, "why have you gone? I am now quite alone! Of Emeralda I am afraid, and Astra does not think of me; she only thinks of the stars. Father, dear, forgive me! I have deceived you. I have travelled through the air on the back of the flying horse. But father, dear, the horse is beautiful, and I love the Chimera! O father dear, I have deceived you, and now I am alone, and I have nobody who cares for me! You are dead, father, and embalmed, and shut up in gold and crystal and jewels, and do not think of your little daughter. Alone! alone! Awe-inspiring is the castle; three hundred towers rise high up in the air. I have never been in all the three hundred, however much I have wandered. O father, father, why have you left me? Who is there to love me now? Who to protect me now in the world? Father, farewell! I will not stay here; I will go away! I will leave the castle. Great is the world and wicked, but Emeralda is powerful and I am afraid of her. If I remain, she will drive me away with her look and shut me up all my life, and my wings I shall break against the unbreakable lattice.

"Father, farewell! I will not remain here. I will flee! Whither? Whither shall I flee? I do not know. O father, dear, alone your child remains in the great, unsafe world! Alone! Alone! O father, farewell, farewell! and forever!"

She rose, she shivered. The dark vaults receded more and more. By the light of the long torches she saw the sacred spiders, which wove web after web; they were never disturbed.

"Sacred spider!" said Psyche to a big fat one, with a cross on its back, "tell me where I must go."

"You cannot flee," replied the spider, high up in the dark vault, in the middle of its web. "Everything is as it is; everything becomes as it was; happens as it happens; all goes to dust. Every day sinks into the deep vaults of the dark pits under us; under us everything becomes the Past, and everything comes into the power of Emeralda. As soon as anything is, it has been, and is in the power of Emeralda. Seek not to flee—that is vanity; submit to your lot. The best thing is that you become one of us, a sacred spider, and weave your web. For our web is sacred; our web is indisturbable; and with all our webs, one for the other, we serve the princess and protect her treasures—the treasure of the Past, which behind our weaving go to dust."

"But if they go to dust, of what value are they?"

"Foolish child, dust is everything. The Past is dust; remembrance is dust. Everything becomes dust; love, jewels—all becomes dust, and the sacred dust we watch over behind our webs. Become a spider like us, weave your web and be wise."

"But I live. I am young, I desire, I love, and I cannot bury myself in dust. . . . Oh, tell me whither I must flee!"

The spider laughed scornfully, and moved its eight legs with great impatience.

"Ask me not about the places of the world—the regions of the wind. I sit here and spin. I am holy. I watch over the treasure of the throne. Disturb me no more with your frivolity, and let not your wings get entangled in the rays of my web, although you are not a moth, but princess of the Kingdom of the Past. . . ."

Psyche was frightened. The spider reverenced her

because she was a princess, but coveted with his wicked instinct.... And she drew back. She cast a last look at the dead face of her father, and fled up the hundred steps. In every corner sat the sacred spiders and moved their legs. Shuddering, she fled on. Whither? She thought of her love, the light-gold Chimera, but nowhere could he be with her for ever. She glided with him through the air, and he brought her back to the castle. His lot was to fly restlessly through the air. Oh, were she but a Chimera like him, had she but two strong wings instead of princesses' wings, she would have gone with him everywhere!...

Whither? Above, from the enthronement-hall, came the sounds of joyful music. There Emeralda was being crowned. Whither? She fled to the terrace.... Oh, if Emeralda missed her, how angry she would be! She would think that Psyche refused to do her homage. She could never return. Farewell, flowers, swans, doves!

The three hundred flags obscured the light. She would never be able to see the Chimera coming. Oh, if he came and she did not see him, and did not beckon to him, and he flew past! He was her only safety! If needs be, she would wait for days together on the battlements. But if Emeralda sent to search for her! Oh, if she did, then there was the cataract; then she would throw herself headlong down, for ever, for ever, into the rushing water with its rainbow colours!

A wind arose. That was the wind that brought her beloved. The flags flapped and impeded her view. And although she saw nothing, she beckoned as in despair, and called out:

"Chimera, Chimera!"

X

IT LIGHTENED. It thundered. Suddenly between the black flags the horse descended.

"What is it, little Psyche?"

"Take me with you."

"Where?"

"Where you like. Take me somewhere. My father is dead. Emeralda reigns. I dare not stay here any longer."

"Get up...."

She got up. He flew away with her. He flew with her the whole day. The sun set; the stars glistened in the dark firmament; and he flew back. Again they approached the castle. The day began to dawn.

"Fly past!" she entreated.

He flew on. Under her she could just see the castle, small as a toy; the three hundred towers, where green flags now fluttered because Emeralda reigned. He flew on.

"Chimera!" she cried. "I love you; you are the most beautiful, most glorious creature that I have ever beheld. Safe I lie upon your back, tied to your mane, my arms round your neck. But I am tired. I am dizzy.

61

I am cold. Put me down somewhere.... Can you not rest with me in a beautiful valley, amongst flowers, near a brook? Are you not thirsty? Will you not graze and lie in a meadow? Do you never, never rest? Chimera, I love you so! But why this restless flying from East to West, from West to East?"

"I must do it, little Psyche."

"Chimera, descend somewhere. Stay somewhere with me. I am tired, I am cold. I want to go to sleep on a bed of moss, under the shadow of trees; sleep there with me."

"I cannot. My lot is to fly through the air, apparently without object, but yet with an object; and what that is, I do not know."

"But what then does the Power want? You fly through the air; the spider spins its web; Emeralda reigns over dust; everything is as it is. Oh, life is comfortless! Chimera, I can hold out no longer! I love you with all my soul, but if you do not descend, then I will loose the knots of your mane, I will let go my arms that are so tired, and then I shall fall down into nothingness...."

"Hold out a little longer. Yonder is the purple desert...."

"Oh, that is beautiful!" she exclaimed. "But you fly past it, always past it!..."

"Do you want to rest Psyche?"

"Oh, yes...."

PSYCHE

"Then I will descend.... Hold out a little longer."
She held him tight, and looked about. He plied his
wings with a rapidity that made her dizzy; they blew a
wind round Psyche....

In the air there loomed the purple sands on the gold-
en sea, with a pearly border of foam; the azure
bananas, which waved their tops in the light-pink
ether....

Psyche held her breath.... "Would he descend
there?..."

Yes, indeed, he was descending. The purple, she
thought, grew pale as soon as he descended; the sea
was no longer golden, the foliage no longer blue....
But yet, yet it was beautiful, a dream-conceit, an
enchanted land, and he was descending. With his
broad wings he glided down. Now he stood still, snorting his breath in a cloud of steam. She glided gently
down his back on to the sand, and laughed, and gave
a sigh of relief!

"Rest now, here, Psyche!" said he dejectedly, and
the quiver in his bronze-sounding voice startled her;
she laughed no more.

"Rest now. Look! here are dates, and there is a
spring. The soft violet night is rapidly spreading over
the sky and cooling the too warm air. A few pale stars
are already glistening. Now quench your thirst; now
refresh yourself and rest.... This is a pleasant oasis.

Now sleep, little Psyche. Tomorrow will soon be here.... Farewell!"

She looked at him with wondering eyes. She threw herself on his broad, powerful, heaving breast, and round his arched neck she threw her trembling arms.

"What?... What do you say, Chimera?" she asked, pale with fear. "What are you going to do? What do you mean? Surely you will rest here with me in the soft violet night and amongst the blue flowers? With me you will refresh yourself with dates and water? You will let me sleep in the shadow of your wings, and watch over me during the dreadful night?"

"No, little Psyche. I am going farther and farther, and then I will return. Then after weeks ... after months, perhaps, you will see me again in the air...."

"You will forsake me?" Here in the desert?"

"Take courage, little Psyche: you are now too tired to fly farther with me through the air. You would slip from my back and fall into nothingness. Here is a pleasant oasis; here are dates and a murmuring stream....

She uttered a cry; her sobs choked her. She uttered a second cry, which frightened the hyenas far away in the desert and made them prick up their ears. She uttered a third, which rent the night-air, and the stars quivered from sympathy.

"Alone!" she cried, and wrung her hands. "Alone! O

Chimera, you will leave me alone with dates and brook! And I thought ... and still hoped, that you would stay with me, king in your country of the rainbow!

"Alone! you will leave me alone in a sandy desert, in nothing but sand, sand in the night, with a single tree and a handful of water! Alone! O Chimera, you cannot do that!... For I love you; I adore you with all my soul, and shall die of grief and tears, Chimera, if you fly away from me! I love you; I worship your golden eyes, your voice of bronze, your steaming breath, your panting flanks, your mane, to which I bound myself, your flaming wings, which carried me far, farther and farther ... to this place!... O Chimera, lay down your smoking limbs in the shadow of the night; lay your noble head in my arms and my bosom, and together we will rest, and tomorrow fly away farther, united forever!"

"I cannot, O little Psyche. I too love you, sweet burden which lay between my wings—little butterfly with weak wings, that lent strength to my flight; but now...."

"But now—O Chimera, but now?..."

"But now I must go, continue my lonely journey to and fro, without knowing why.... Farewell, little Psyche, hope in life, hope in the morrow...."

He spread his wings, his limbs quivered, he ascended into the air.

She wrung her arms, her hands. She sobbed, she sobbed....

"Have pity!" she implored. "Pity, pity! What have I done? Why do you punish me so? My God, what have I done? I have trusted, hoped, given my soul in happiness.... Is happiness then punished? Is it not good to hope, to trust, and to love? Ought I then to have mistrusted and hated? What do I ask? He no longer hears me! What do I care for the problems of life! Him I love, and in me is nothing but my love and despair, and round me is the desert and the night, and now ... now I must die!"

She sobbed, and her tears flowed. She was alone. Around her loomed the night, around her stretched the sands as far as the perceptible horizon. And above her glistened the stars.

And she wept. Her grief was too great for her little soul. She wept.

"Alone!" she sobbed. "Alone!... I will not quench my thirst, I will not refresh myself, nor will I sleep. I am tired, but I will go on...."

On she went, and wept. In the night she walked on through the sand, and she wept. She wept from fear and despair. And she wept so, her tears flowed so many, down her cheeks that they fell, her tears, like drops, great and warm, deep into the sand. Her tears flowed down into the sand. Her tears flowed down into the sand. And she wept, she kept weeping, and as she went along . . . her tears did not stop. Then in the sand, her tears so warm and so great, formed little lakes. And as she went and kept going on and weeping, the little lakes flowed into one another, and behind her flowed a stream of tears. Meandering after her flowed her tears. And on she went in the night and wept. . . . After her, meandered faithfully the stream of her tears. . . . And she thought of her lost happiness. . . . He had forsaken her. . . . Why? . . . She had loved him so, still loved him so. . . . Oh, she would always love him so—always, always!

And in her love she did not scold him. For she loved him and scolded not. She longed for no revenge, for she loved him. . . .

"That was fate," she thought, weeping. "He could not do anything else. He was obliged. . . ."

She wept. And oh! she was so tired, so tired of the wide sky, so tired of the wide sand! Then she thought she could go no farther, and should fall into the stream of her tears. . . . But before her a lofty shadow fell with gloomy darkness on the violet night. She looked up, and had to strain her neck to see to the top of the shadow. The shadow was round above, and then tapered off behind. . . . But she wept so, that she did not see. . . . Then with her hand she wiped away the tears from her eyes and gazed. . . . The shadow was awful, like that of an awfully great beast. And she kept wiping away her tears, which formed a pool around her, and gazed. . . .

Then she saw. She saw, squatting in the sand, a terribly great beast like a lion, immovable. The beast was as great as a castle, high as a tower; its head reached to the stars. But its head was the head of a woman, slender, enveloped in a basalt veil, which fell down, right and left, along her shoulders. And the woman's head stood on the breast of a woman, two breasts of a gigantic woman, of basalt. But the body, that squatted down in the sand, was a lion, and the forepaws protruded like walls.

The night shone. The sultry night shone with diamonds over the horizonless desert. And in the starlight night the beast, terrible, rested there, half-woman, half-lion, squatting in the sand, its paws extended and its breasts and woman's head protruding, gigantic, reaching to the stars. Her basalt eyes stared straight before her. Her mouth was shut and so were the basalt lips, which would never speak.

Psyche stood before the beast. Around her was the night; around her was the sand; above her the diamond, shining stars. Silently shuddering and full of awe, stood Psyche. Then she thought: "It must be she, the Sphinx. . . ."

She wept. Her tears flowed; She stood in the stream of her tears, which, winding along, followed her. And

weeping, she lifted up her voice, small in the night—
the voice of a child that speaks in the illimitable.

"Awful Sphinx," she said, "make me wise. You
know the problem of life. I pray you solve it for me,
and let me no longer weep. . . ."

The Sphinx was silent.

"Sphinx," continued Psyche, "open your stony lips.
Speak! Tell me the riddle of life. I was born a princess,
naked, with wings; I cannot fly. The light-gold
Chimera, the splendid horse with the silver wings,
came down to me, took me away with him in wanderings through the air, and I loved him. He has left me—
me, a child—alone in the desert, alone in the night.
Tell me why? If I know, I shall—perhaps—weep no
more. Sphinx, I am tired. I am tired of the air, tired of
the sand, tired from crying. And I cannot stop; I keep
on crying. If you do not speak to me, Sphinx, then I
will drown you, gigantic as you are, in my tears. Look
at them flowing around me; look at them rippling at
your feet like a sea. Sphinx, they will rise above your
head. Sphinx, speak!"

The Sphinx was silent.

The Sphinx, with stony eyes, looked away into the
night of diamond stars. Her basalt lips remained
closed.

And Psyche wept. Then she cast a look at the stars.

"Sacred Stars," she murmured, "I am alone. My

father is dead. The Chimera has gone. The Sphinx is silent. I am alone, and afraid and tired. Sacred Stars, watch over me. See my tears no longer flow; for this night they are exhausted.... I can cry no more. I will go to sleep, here, between the feet of the Sphinx. She speaks not, it is true; but—perhaps she is not angry, and if she wants to crush me with her foot, I care not. But yet I will go to sleep between her powerful feet. In your looks of living diamond, I feel compassion thrill.... Sacred Stars, I will go to sleep; watch over me...."

She lay down between the feet of the Sphinx, against the breast of the Sphinx. And she was so little and the Sphinx so great, that she was like a butterfly sitting near a tower.

Then she fell asleep.

The night was very still. Far, far away in the boundless desert, a mist drifted horizonlessly along, and lit up the darkness. The stream of Psyche's tears meandered, like a silver thread, far away from whence she had come. She herself slept. The Sphinx, with staring eyes and closed mouth, looked out high into the night. The stars twinkled and watched.

XI

WITHOUT A CLOUD arose on the horizon the first dawn of day, the round, rosy-coloured morning glimmer. And in the dawn appeared the horizon, and bordered the sandy plain.

In the rosy light, gigantic, towered the gloomy Sphinx. Psyche slept.... But through her weary eyelids, the light softly sent its rays, coral-red, and she suddenly awoke.... She opened her eyes, but did not move.

She remained in her slumbering attitude, but her eyes looked about. She saw the desert, without an oasis, only the brooklet of tears that meandered far away from whence she had come. It was like a silver thread in the rosy light of the dawn, and she followed its windings with her eyes as long as she could. And when she thus looked, she began to weep again. The tears fell on the feet of the Sphinx, and Psyche wept, in her slumbering position. There was a mist before her eyes, and through the mist glimmered the rosy desert and the little glistening stream.

But now she wiped away her tears, which trickled through her fingers, for she thought she saw ... and that was so improbable. She wiped her eyes again, and saw. She thought she saw ... and it was so improbable.... But yet it was so: she saw. She saw someone coming; along every winding of the brook, she saw someone approaching.... Who was it coming there? She knew not.... He came nearer and nearer. Was she dreaming? No she was awake. He came, whoever he was. He was approaching....

She remained sitting in the same attitude. And he came nearer and nearer, following the briny track, till he stood before the Sphinx. The Sphinx was so great and Psyche so little, that at first he did not see her. But because she was so white, with crimson wings, he saw her, a little thing red and white!

He approached between the feet of the Sphinx till he stood right before her.

He approached reverentially, because she had wept so much. When he was quite close, he knelt down and folded his hands.

Through her tears she did not recognise him.

"Who are you?" she asked in a faint voice.

He stood up and approached still closer, and then she recognised him. He was Prince Eros, the King of the Present.

"I know who you are," said Psyche. "You are Prince Eros, who was to have married Emeralda, or Astra."

He smiled, and she said:

"Why do you come here into the desert? Are you seeking here for the Jewel, or the Glass that magnifies?"

He smiled, and shook his head.

"No, Psyche," he said gently. "I have never sought for the Jewel nor for the Glass.

"But first tell me: why are you here and sleeping by the Sphinx?"

She told him. She spoke of her father who was dead, of the light-gold Chimera, of the purple desert and the sorrowful night. She told him of her tears.

"I have followed them. O Psyche!" he replied. "I have come ever since I saw you before your father's throne—a day never to be forgotten!

"I have come here every day. Every day I leave my garden of the Present, to ask the awful Sphinx for the solution of my problem."

"What problem, Prince Eros?"

"The problem of my grief. For I am grieved about you, Psyche, because you would not follow me and stayed with your father.... Now I know why. You loved the Chimera...."

She blushed, and hid her face in her hands.

"Who could see the Chimera and not love him more than me?" said Eros gently. "Who could love him, and not weep over him?" he whispered still more gently; but she did not hear him.

Then he spoke louder.

"Every morning, Psyche, I come to ask the Sphinx how long I must suffer, and why I must suffer. And still much more, O Psyche, I ask the Sphinx, what I will not tell you now, because...."

"Because?..."

"Because it would perhaps pain you to hear the question of my heart. So I came now, O Psyche, and then I espied a brooklet meandering through the sand. I did not know it; I was thirsty, for I am always thirsty. I stooped down and scooped up the clear water in my hand. It tasted salt, Psyche: they were tears."

"My tears ..." she said, and wept.

"Psyche, I drank them. Tell me, do you forgive me for that?"

"Yes...."

"I followed the brook, and now I have found you."

She was silent; she looked at him. He knelt down by her.

"Psyche," said he gently, "I love you. Because I saw you little and naked and winged, standing amongst your proud sisters—Psyche, I love you. I love you so much, that I would weep all your tears for you, and would give you ... the Chimera."

"You can't do that," she said sadly.

"No, Psyche," answered he, "that cannot alas be done. I can only weep for myself; and the Chimera ... nobody can catch him."

"He flies too fast," she said, "and he is much too strong; but it is very kind of you, Prince Eros...."

She stretched out her hand, and he kissed it reverentially.

Then he looked at her for a long time.

"Psyche," said he, gently "will the Sphinx give me an answer to my question this morning?"

She cast down her eyes.

"Psyche," he went on, "I have drunk your tears; I respect your grief, too great for your little heart. But may I suffer it with you? O Psyche, little Psyche, little, in the great desert, now your father is dead, now the Chimera is away, now you are all alone.... O Psyche, now come with me! Oh, let me now love you! O Psyche, come now with me! Psyche, alone in the desert, a little butterfly in a sandy plain—Psyche, on, come with me! I will give you a summer-house to live in, a garden to play in, and all my love to comfort you. Don't despise them. All that I have will I give! Small is my palace and small my garden round it, but greater than the desert and the sky is my great love. O Psyche, come with me now! Then you will suffer cold and hunger and thirst no more, and the grief that your heart now suffers, Psyche, ... we will bear together."

He stretched out his arms. She smiled, tired and pale from weeping, slid from the foot of the Sphinx, and nestled to his heart.

"Eros," she murmured, "I suffer. I pine. I weep. I gave away all that I had. I have nothing more than my grief. Can grief ... be happiness in the Present?"

He smiled.

"From grief ... comes happiness," he answered. "From grief ... will come happiness, not in the present, but ... in the Future!"

She looked at him inquiringly.

"What is that" she asked. "Future!... It is a very sweet work.... I do not know what it is, but I have heard it before.... Father sometimes spoke of it with an affected voice.... It seems to be something far away, far, far away.... From grief will come ... in the Future ... happiness!

"Far behind me lies the Past.... Then I was a child. Now I am a woman.... A woman.... Now I am, Eros, a woman, a woman who has wept and suffered, and asked of the silent Sphinx.... Now I am no longer a princess, but a woman, a queen ... of the Present!..."

She fell against his shoulder and fainted. He gave a sign, and out of the air flew a glittering golden chariot, drawn by two panting griffons. He lifted her into the chariot. He held her tight in his arm, and pressed her to his heart. With his other hand he guided his two dragon-winged lions through the glowing air of the desert.

XII

WHEN PSYCHE opened her eyes, she heard the soft music of two pipes. And she awoke from her swoon with a smile. She lay still and did not move, but looked about her. She was reclining upon a soft bed of purple, on a couch of ivory. She lay in a crystal palace; round the palace were pillars of crystal and a round crystal gallery. The pillars were entwined with roses, willow, white, and pink, and they perfumed the sunny spring morning. Through the gallery of pillars, through the walls of crystal, she saw round her a pleasant meadow, like a round valley, a valley like a garden, through which ran a murmuring brook between beds of flowers. Quite near appeared the horizon of a low hill-slope, and the cloudless sky was like a chalice of turquoise.

The pipes changed their music. Psyche raised herself a little higher, leaning on her arm; she laughed and looked about. In the middle of the crystal palace was a basin of white marble, full of water, and doves were hopping about it or drinking. Sitting at the gate of crystal pillars, Psyche saw two girls; with their fingers they raised the flutes to their mouth and played.

Psyche laughed and listened. Then she fell back on the bed again, happy, but tired, full of rest and contentment, and she raised her head and looked up!...

Through a crocus-coloured curtain fell the tempered spring sunshine, quiet and soft, joyous and still.

Psyche breathed more freely, and a sigh escaped from her heart. She put her arms under her head; her wings lay stretched out right and left on either side of her, and when she heard the music of the flutes, her thoughts drifted away like an aimless dream, like rose-leaves upon water.

She dreamed and she listened.... She no longer felt tired, and her eyes, which had shed a brook of tears, felt moist and fresh, cooled by an invisible hand, with invisible care. Her breathing was regular, and her soul felt safe.... And she smiled continually....

The pipes ceased playing....

The two girls, seeing that the queen had awakened, rose up and approached her bed with a basket of red-blushing fruit, which they set down near her. Then they made a deep reverence, but spoke not, and sat down again by the pillars and blew their pipes anew; but to another tune, somewhat louder, like a voice calling, and both in unison. The pipes sounded jubilant in the morning, and outside, high in the air, the lark answered joyously....

Psyche smiled, stretched out her hand and took a

peach, a pear, a bunch of blue grapes. The pipes played merrily together, and higher and higher and higher soared the lark and sang. Then Psyche heard the brook babbling gently; the doves answered one another, and round her the morning sang her welcome.

Then footsteps light approached her softly; the pipes ceased playing; the girls rose and made a deep reverence. And between the pillars of crystal appeared Prince Eros, the King of the Present.

The girls withdrew, and Eros approached and knelt before Psyche.

He said nothing, but looked at her.

"Eros," said Psyche, "I thank you.... I have rested; my eyes cease to burn; my hunger is appeased.... I have heard sweet music, and everything appeared kind and to love me."

"Everything in my kingdom is glad that the queen has come. Everything is glad that the queen has awakened."

"The Queen of the Present," murmured Psyche.

Then she put her arm round his neck, and leant her head against his shoulder. "Eros," said she gently, "I love you.... How shall I express my love to you! You have walked in the track of my tears, my salt tears you have drunk; out of the desert, from the breast of the awful Sphinx, you lifted me in your chariot, drawn by swift griffons.... In my swoon I felt myself going through the air, not with the speed of the fair Chimera, whose hoofs struck lightning and made the thunder roll high in the ether ... but smoothly and evenly on wheels, over the clouds delicately tinted with the glowing dawn. How long did we travel?... How long have I slept? Eros, how shall I express my love to you! My love is deep gratitude, inexpressible, because you rescued me. My love is heartfelt thankfulness, because you have cared for and refreshed me. My love is...."

She paused for a moment, and rose from the bed.

"What, Psyche?" said he gently, and stood up.

"My love is deep, submissive respect, O Eros, because you wanted to weep my tears and give me the wish of my heart, which, had it been fulfilled, would have caused you the most poignant grief."

She sank upon her knees and took his hand in hers and kissed it long. He lifted her up and pressed her to his breast.

"My gentle Psyche!" said he. "My child and my wife and my tender princess! Kneel not to me. In love it is sweet to give and to suffer. Love gives, and love suffers...."

"I have only suffered, but not given," said Psyche, in a low tone.

"To suffer is to give most. To give to one we love the suffering of his suffering soul, is the greatest gift that can be given, my child and my princess! Try, with the remembrance sacred to Suffering and Love, endured and loved, to be happy in the Present. Oh, let the Past be a remembrance, a sacred remembrance, a golden remembrance; but now look to the Present. Oh, let the Present comfort you—the present, little, humble and poor. Look! This is all. This cupola is my palace, this garden is my kingdom; these flowers and these birds, they are all my treasures—roses and doves and the singing lark. More I have not; but I have still my love—my love, great as the heaven and wide as the universe. But he who lives in love so great, needs no greater palace and no greater kingdom to rule over. For the treasures of Emeralda I would not exchange my kingdom and my love. . . . Psyche, my queen, yet I have ornaments for you. The Princess of Nakedness with the wings may never wear jewels of precious stones, and jewels I have not. But pearls, Psyche, I have pearls which Emeralda despises. Pearls, Psyche, I found in your tears of yesterday. See! I strung them together, they were a crown for you. Pearls may adorn you, tears may adorn you, my child of suffering, my wife of love, queen of my soul and of my kingdom. . . ."

Then he took a little crown of twelve great pearls and put it on her head. Then he hung a necklace of pearls round her neck. And as she stood before him naked, so immaculately delicate in her princessly nakedness, he threw around her loins a light, thin veil, richly adorned with pearls, and which she fastened in a knot. Then he gave her a mirror, and she beheld herself very beautiful, crowned like a queen, and smiled with contentment.

"Am I a queen?" she said softly. "Am I happy? Eros, do you love me? Is this the happiness of the Present? Eros, do I love you out of gratitude and respect, my husband and my king?..."

He led her gently away, through the porticos, down the crystal steps. Cupids hovered about them, the lark sang high in the heavens, the roses perfumed the air, the brook murmured gently. The spring rejoiced to welcome them, and behind the shrubs the pipes played a duet. The hill-slope of the horizon was peaceful, and above, the heavens, arched like a turquoise chalice.

Everything sang, everything was fragrant; in the grass buzzed thousands of insects; about the flowers fluttered butterflies; and where Psyche, on her husband's arm, walked along the flower beds, all the flowers bowed to her in homage—the white slender lilies, the violets with laughing eyes, tall flowers and short flowers, on long and short stems—and all gave forth their fragrance.

Eros pointed around.

"This is the Present, Psyche," said he, and pressed her to his heart.

"And this is happiness, that is as a lily and a violet," she whispered, with her lips to his.

XIII

THE PLEASANT DAYS followed each other like a row of laughing houris.... Eros and Psyche tended the flowers, which did not fade when Psyche stroked the stems or gently kissed the calyces. They wandered along the brook, and, if the days were warm, sought coolness under the crocus-coloured awning, in the crystal palace, where the doves cooed round the basin. The flutes played, or Eros himself took a lyre and sang, at Psyche's feet, the stories of days gone by.

It was one of the pleasures of the flower-laughing Present.

Between the shrubs, where May strewed fragrant snow-blossom, naked, chubby cupids with tender wings played or romped, hovering like little clouds in the air.

The sweet nights followed the pleasant days; the diamond stars, the same which Psyche had entreated to watch over her in the desert, glittered in the heavens. Under the roses, close to one another, slumbered the fair-winged children, tired out with play, their little mouths open and their chubby legs all folds. The air was heavy with the breath of lilac and jasmine; it was spring, it was the Present, it was night!...

And while Psyche lay with her head against Eros's shoulder and he wound his arm round her waist, while Psyche looked up at the stars sacred in the violet night, the nightingale broke out into melody. The bird sang, and sang alone; everything was still. The bird sang, and let her notes fall in the air like drops of sprinkled sound, like the harmonious falling of water from a playing fountain. The bird sang, and Psyche closed her eyes, and felt on her lips Eros's kiss.

The days followed the nights. It was always the sweet pleasure of flowers and birds, of spring and love, cupids and roses, music and dance. The flowers were more beautiful, and did not fade; the fruits were sweeter and of richer colour; the spring air was lighter, and life was happier than a golden day. It was day which lasted days and nights; it was the Present.

If Psyche were alone she longed for Eros, and when she saw him again she spread out her arms, and they loved each other. If Psyche were alone, she wandered about in the rosy spring morning; the flowers bowed down to her; the brook flowed cool over her feet; she played with the winged cherubs, who flew about her head like butterflies; she sat down in the moss full of violets; she bade the children take off her crown, loosen the plaits of her long hair, untie the knots of the drapery round her loins, and she lay down on the bank of the rook; her hand played with the clear cold water, and, naked in the shade of flowery shrubs, she fell asleep and the cupids round her. Then the footstep of the king awoke her; the children awoke; they dressed her, and she went to meet her husband, and received him with open arms. It was the sweet delight of the Present.

One day she was sleeping naked under the shrubs, the boys round her; on the moss lay her crown and her veil, and the brooklet flowed on, gently murmuring. The day was very still, heavy with warmth. A storm was brewing, but the sky was still blue. In the far-off distance, where the horizon was like waves of the sea, clouds pregnant with storm curled up gloomily like ostrich feathers. And once there was lightning, but no thunder.

Then above the ridge of the hill something dark appeared to rise against the stormy clouds. It was round like a head, like a black head. From the black head leered two eyes, black as jet, and nothing more appeared. Long leered the eyes; then from the palace a voice cried.

"Psyche, Psyche!"

Psyche awoke, and the cupids with her. Eros approached and led her away. The air grew dark, and the next moment the summer storm burst forth, dark sky, lightning, rain and thunder rapidly rolling on. It lasted only for a time; then the sky became blue again, the flowers recovered their breath and raised their drooping heads, shaking with fresh rain.

XIV

NEXT DAY, WHEN Psyche was sleeping again by the brook, the dark head with leering eyes of jet appeared again on the horizon. For a long time the eyes leered, full of lust. Then the head rose up higher like a dark sun, behind the hill-slope in the sky.

It was a face tanned by the sun, with coal-black hair; round the temples a wreath of vine leaves, and from the wreath protruded two horns like those of a young goat.

The eyes looked lustful and young, as though they were jet and gold. The lips laughed in the curly beard, and the sharp teeth were dazzling white; the pointed ears stood up.

Then the dark face became perfectly visible in the light; the shoulders rose brown and naked, and two brown hands with long fingers lifted to the lips a pipe of short and long reeds. The pipe played a fanfare, a march of very quick notes. Then it stopped, and the gold-jet eyes leered. Psyche moved in her sleep. Then the pipe sounded again, and Psyche opened her eyes. Astonished, she listened to the notes of the pipe, as they rose and fell as she had never heard before, lively and wanton, quick and playful. She sat up, leant on her arm, and looked. . . .

She started. There, on the horizon, like a dark sun, she saw the grown face and the lips in the curly beard blowing the reeds, short and long. Psyche started and looked on trembling. Then the pipe stopped again, and roguishly the head nodded to her. Psyche was frightened; she woke the boys. She fled away. From the palace Eros came to meet her.

At first she meant to speak, but he kissed her; and why, she did not know, but she spoke not. Then she made up her mind to tell Eros that night, but in her husband's arms she lacked the courage to speak. She did not tell him. The next morning she resolved not to repose again on the moss by the brook. But that after-noon she played with the cupids, and tired, fell asleep in the same place. The pipe awoke her; on the horizon, the grown face stood out against the sun, and roguish-ly nodded to her.

Psyche, indignant, looked up.

The head rose, the shoulders rose, and the whole form then rose up: a sunburnt youth, with the legs of a goat, rough-haired and cloven hoofs. There he stood, his dark shadow reflected in the golden rays of the set-ting sun. He blew his reeds; he piped lustily and mer-rily, roguishly and joyously and as well as he could, to please Psyche. She listened—about her the boys were sleeping—and she smiled. He saw her smile and smiled too. Then proudly she pointed with her finger for him to go. He went, but the next day he was there again. Then she saw him every day. He stood in the sun, which was going down, and blew his reeds, laughed and nodded to her roguishly. Sometimes Psyche bade him be gone; sometimes she pretended not to see who was playing there; sometimes she listened graciously. When she heard the king call:

"Psyche! Psyche!" she woke the cupids, who dressed her in a moment, and went to meet her husband. She kissed him, and wished to tell him that every day a young man with goat's legs stood on the hill and played upon his pipe. But because she had kept silent so long, she was silent again, and could not open her lips. It made her sad, and Eros saw her sadness, and often asked her what it was that disturbed the equanimity of her soul. She said "*Nothing*," and embraced him and declared that she was happy. But when the lark warbled and the nightingale's sweet notes were heard, when Eros sang to the lyre and the brook murmured gently, Psyche always heard, between the pleasant sounds, the impudent tunes of the reeds, short and long. She tried not to hear, but she always heard them. They sounded saucily and merrily, like the sounds of a little bird in a wood calling something to her from afar; she heard, but did not yet understand what.

One day, when he stood in the same place blowing lustily with puffed-out cheeks, Psyche, indignant, rose with her lips closely pressed together. She put her veil on and wound it tightly round her loins, without waking the boys. Then with a firm step and innocently, she crossed a little slope, and came into a valley, a valley of grass; there the brook flowed away between multitudes of irises and narcissi. The goat, leering and laughing, tripped nimbly down the hill on his hoofs to meet her.

"Who are you?" said Psyche haughtily.

"I am the Satyr," said he deferentially. "And now will you just see me dance?"

He piped a waltz, and danced for her to the measure of his tripping music. He turned on his feet, spun round and round, and underneath, on his back, she saw his tiny tail wagging. She laughed, and found him amusing, with his tail, and feet, and horns. Then he turned a somersault, and finished his dance with a bow.

"You may not come here," said Psyche severely. "This is the Kingdom of the Present, and I am the queen, and my husband Eros, the king of the kingdom. You dance indeed nicely, and you play rather pretty tunes, but you may not come here. We have here the lark and the nightingale, and my husband sings to the lyre."

"That is classical music," said the Satyr.

90

"I don't know what you mean by *classical music*. But you may not come here and pipe, and disturb me in my afternoon slumber. If my husband knew it, he would be very angry, and have you torn to pieces by two raging griffons."

"I am not afraid of that," said the Satyr. "Why, I tame panthers, and they are much more dangerous."

"I had pity on you," continued Psyche severely, raising her head in queenly dignity, "and have not yet said anything to the king. But if you come again tomorrow, I will tell him."

"No, you won't!" said the Satyr saucily.

"You are an ill-mannered boy!" said Psyche, angry and offended. "You must not speak so to a princess. I ought not to condescend to speak to you. I can see very well that you don't know how people behave at court, and that you come from the wood. And you are ugly, too, with your hairy feet and your tail."

The Satyr looked at her astonished.

"I think you very pretty!" he whispered admiringly. "Oh, I think you so pretty! You have such pretty eyes, and such golden hair, and such a white skin! Only, I don't like your wings. The nymphs haven't any."

"You may not speak to me like that!" said Psyche vexed. "I am the queen. How dare you? Go away now, else I will call the wild beasts here."

"Well, don't be angry!" said the Satyr in a low,

imploring tone. "That is my way of speaking. We all speak like that in the wood. The Bacchantes, too, are not particular what they say. We are unacquainted with your court language. And we don't know anything of classical music. But we are always very merry and sociable together; but you must come once...."

"Are you going?" said Psyche imperiously, and red with passion, and with her finger she pointed to him to be gone. He crouched down suddenly in the reeds of the brook among the irises and narcissi, and she saw him stealing away through the high grass. When she turned round she beheld the cupids; they were bringing her her crown.

"The king is looking for you, Psyche!" they cried out in the distance, and like a cloud they hovered round her.

She went back with them and threw herself into the arms of her husband.

"Don't roam so far away, my little Psyche!" said Eros. "In the wood behind the hills are wild beasts...."

Night came on; Eros sang, the nightingale filled the air with her sweet notes.

"Classical music!" thought Psyche.

XV

PSYCHE HAD A SECRET. Why did she not tell it? She did not know. She could not, after having once kept silent. She knew that she was not doing right by being silent, and yet she did not speak. But she was very sad about it, and felt dissatisfied. Then she wanted to speak with Eros; but because she had said nothing at first, she was afraid. And then she said to herself: "The Satyr does nothing wrong by standing there and piping a little, and it is not worthwhile thinking much about it...."

And yet she *did* think about it, and in her ears she always heard his saucy voice, his coarse words, countrified and funny.

Then she laughed about it all.

"But what does he do—what is he? A Satyr? What is a Satyr? What are Bacchantes? And what are nymphs? Panthers, too, I have never seen. I should like to see them. What is their life there in the wood? There are many lives in the world, and most of them are a secret. I only know the courtiers of the Kingdom of the Past.... Here there are the two girls that play on the pipe and the winged children. I should like to see all that there is in the world, and experience all that is in life. There must be strange things, which I never see.... The Chimera was glorious, and deep in my soul I always long for him; but in other respects everything is the same.... No wonders take place in this garden.... Eros is a young prince; then there are the doves, the griffons, the cupids.... That is all so commonplace.... Oh, to seek, to wander! The world is so great! The universe is awful, although it has limits. My father said it had no limits.... Oh, if it had no limits!... Oh, to seek, to wander, to soar in the air!.... I shall never see the Chimera again. Never shall I soar in the air again.... He conjured up visions for me, and then let them pass away.... Oh, to soar through the air! When shall I see him again, and when shall I soar again?... Eros I love—he is my husband; but he has no wings. The Chimera had powerful wings of silver feathers. He has left me for ever...."

So, alone with her thought, she wandered in the garden. The cupids she drove away, and, crying, they hid themselves among the roses. When the Satyr appeared, she went to meet him in the valley, where the irises were blooming.

"So, you are there again!"

"Yes! Won't you just see me dance again?"

He danced and frisked his tail.

"I have already told you more than once that you may not come here," said Psyche severely.

He winked roguishly; he knew very well that his presence was not disagreeable to her.

"You are so beautiful!" he said, in his most flattering tone; "much more beautiful than any of the nymphs."

"And the Bacchantes, then?" said Psyche.

"Much more beautiful than the Bacchantes!" he answered. "But they are also very nice. Tell me, wouldn't you like to see them?"

Psyche was very inquisitive, and he noticed it.

"Won't you just see them?" the Satyr repeated temptingly.

"Where?" said Psyche.

"Look ... there!" He pointed in the distance with his finger.

On the hill Psyche saw forms madly whirling round in a dance.

"Those are the Bacchantes!" said the Satyr. Psyche laughed.

"How madly they whirl round!" she exclaimed. "Are they always so merry?"

"Oh, we are always dancing," said the Satyr. "In the wood it is always pleasure. We play at tag with one another, we drink the juice of the grapes, and we dance till nightfall."

"Psyche! Psyche!" called a voice.

It was her husband. The Satyr fled through the flags, and Psyche hastened back.

She threw herself into Eros's arms, who asked her where she had been. And without answering him, she began to cry and hid her face in his breast.

"What is it, little Psyche?" asked Eros. "Are you in trouble? Amongst the roses the boys cry, and by the brook the queen cries. Is there then sadness in my kingdom? Does not Psyche feel happy?"

She wept and shrugged her shoulders, as if to say that she did not know. And she hid her face in his breast.

"Tell me, Psyche, what is the matter?"

She would have liked to tell him, but she could not; a stronger power kept her back.

"Does not Psyche feel happy? Does she long for the Chimera?"

She laid her little hand upon his lips.

"Don't speak about him. I am not worthy of him. I am not worthy of you, Eros."

He kissed her very gently.

"What does my Psyche think about? May I not leave her any more, alone by the brook?"

"No, no!" said she hastily, and drew his arms round her.... "No," she continued quickly. "Don't leave me alone any more. Always stay by me. Protect me from myself, O Eros!..."

"Is little Psyche ill?"

She nodded in the affirmative, and laid her burning

head upon his breast; she nestled against him and shut her feverish eyes.

He stayed by her, and all around was still and the cupids appeared fluttering in the air. That night she slept in Eros's arms. She awoke for a moment out of her sleep; far away in the distance through the crystal of the palace she heard the sound of pipes. She raised her head and listened. But she would not hear any more, and hid herself in Eros's arms and fell asleep on his heart.

The next day he stayed by her, and they wandered to the brook. Sadness hung over the garden, the flowers drooped. In the afternoon Psyche became uneasy; she heard the pipe, and in the distance caught a glimpse of vague forms dancing.

"Do you see nothing?" she asked Eros.

"No...."

"Do you hear nothing?" she said again.

"No," he answered. "Poor Psyche is ill. And the flowers are ill too, because she is. Oh, let Eros cure you!..."

The following night, in the arms of her husband, she heard the pipe. It played saucy, short, lively tunes. "Come, come, now dance with us; we are drinking the grapes. Come ... come!..."

She could resist no longer. Trembling, she loosed herself from her husband's arms, who was asleep. She got up, stole out of the palace, fled through the garden to the alluring voice.

The flowers in the brook seemed to entreat her: "Oh, go not away! Oh, go not away!" The nightingale uttered a cry, and she thought it was an owl.

She hurried on to the valley, where the irises were in blossom. There, near the brook, in the light of the moon, stood the Satyr, tripping to the sound of his pipe, and round him, hand in hand, madly danced the Bacchantes, naked, a panther's skin cast about them, their wild streaming hair encircled with vine-leaves. They danced like drunken spectres in the pale moonlight night; they waved their thyrsus, and pelted each other with grapes, which smashed to juice upon their faces.

"Come, come!" they cried triumphantly.

Psyche was startled by their voices, rough and hoarse. But they opened their circle, two stretched their hand out to Psyche, and they danced round with her. The wild dance excited her; she had never known till then what dancing was, and she danced with sparkling eyes. She waved a thyrsus, and pressed the grapes to her mouth. . . . Then suddenly the Satyr caught hold of her and kissed her passionately, pressing the grapes to her lips. . . .

"Psyche! Psyche!"

She started and stood still. The Bacchantes, the Satyr, fled.

Psyche hastened back; with her hand she wiped her contaminated, burning lips.

". . . Psyche!"

She ran to meet Eros, but when she saw him, god-like and beautiful as an image, spotlessly pure in the moonlight, with his noble countenance, his deep brown eyes full of love, she was so disgusted with herself that she fell at his feet in a swoon.

He lifted her up and laid her on the bed.

He watched while she slumbered.

The whole night he watched by her. . . .

And it seemed as if she were wandering in her mind. . . . Her face glowed with fever, and ever and anon she wiped her lips.

Outside in the garden the flowers drooped in sorrow. The lark was silent, and the little angels sat together with their wings drawn in. The sky was ash-coloured and gloomy.

That night Psyche slept in Eros's arms, and afar off the pipe allured her. . . .

She extracted herself from Eros's embrace and got up. . . .

She wanted to kiss him for the last time, but dared not, for fear of waking him.

"Farewell!" she whispered very gently. "Noble Eros, beloved husband, farewell! I am unworthy of you. The Satyr's kiss is still burning on my lips; my mouth is on fire from the juice of the grapes. Farewell!... And if you can, forgive me!"

She went.

The night was sultry and heavy with thunder; the flowers, exhausted, hung their heads; the nightingale uttered a cry, and she thought it was an owl. Bats flitted about with flapping wings.

She walked with a firm step. She followed the brook to where it flowed into the valley. Yonder ... with the Satyr in their midst, danced the Bacchantes.

Hurrah! Hurrah!" they cried out, rough and hoarse, and threw at her a bunch of grapes.

She hesitated a moment.... She raised her eyes. Through the gloomy night a single star glistened like a cold, proud eye.

"Sacred star!" said Psyche, "you who watched over me before, and now leave me for ever ... tell him that I am unworthy of him and beg him to forgive me!"

The star hid itself in the darkness.

"Come!" cried the Bacchantes.

Psyche took a step forward....

"Brook!" she then cried, "little stream of the land of the Present, babbling pure and peacefully, in which I never more may cool myself ... oh, tell him that I am unworthy of him and beg him to forgive me!"

The brook went murmuring over the stones, and muttered: "No, no...."

"Come, come!" cried the Bacchantes.

Then Psyche plucked a single violet, white as a maiden's face.

"Sweet violet!" said she "humble flower, don't be proud. Your queen, who is forsaking her kingdom, entreats the star and brook in vain. She is no longer a queen. She is no longer obeyed. Sweet violet, hear the prayer of Psyche, who, unworthy, is forsaking the Present...."

"Stay, Psyche!" implored the flower in her hand.

"Dear little flower!" said Psyche, "born in the moss, withering when you are plucked, what do you know of gods and mortals? What do you know of soul and life and power? Psyche can no longer stay. But beg Love to forgive her!... Oh, give him my last message!"

She kissed the flower and laid it in the moss.

"Psyche! Psyche! Come!" cried the Bacchantes.

She sprang forward into the midst of the dance.

"Here I am!" she cried wildly. And they dragged her away with them to the wood.

XVI

WHEN EROS AWOKE that morning, he found not Psyche by his side. He got up, thinking that she was in the garden, and went out. The sky was dull and lowering, a mist hung over the hills. The lark had not sung, the cupids were not fluttering about.

"Psyche!" cried he, "Psyche!"

No answer was returned. No sigh rustled in the leaves of the trees; no insect hummed in the grass; the flowers hung down withered on their limp stems. A deathly chilliness reigned around. A fearful presentiment took possession of Eros. He walked along the flower-beds, along the brook.

"Oh! where is Psyche?" he cried. "Oh, tell me, water, flowers, birds, where is Psyche!"

No answer was returned. The brook flowed on murkily and noiselessly, the flowers lay across the path; no bird sang among the leaves. He wrung his hands and hastened on. Then he came to the spot where Psyche was wont to rest in the moss by the brook, in the shade of the shrubs.

"Who will tell me where Psyche is?" he exclaimed in despair, and threw himself on the moss and sobbed.

"Eros!" cried a weak voice.

"Who speaks there?"

"I, a white violet, which Psyche plucked.... Hear me quickly, for I feel I am dying, and my elfin voice is scarcely audible to your ear. Listen to me.... I am lying close to you. Take me in your hand...."

Eros took the flower.

"Psyche has been enticed by the Satyr into the wood. The Bacchantes have taken her away. This was her last word: that she was unworthy of you, and went away praying for forgiveness. She could not remain, she said; she went!... Eros, forgive her!"

The flower shrivelled up in his hand. Eros rose and tottered; he too felt that he was dying.

Sad at heart walked Eros, and all along his path the flowers now lay shrivelled. The brook was dry. The lark lay dead before his feet. The cupids lay dead in the withered roses.

Eros went into the castle and fell upon the purple bed.

A single dove was expiring at the marble basin.

The strings of the lyre were all broken....

Eros too felt that his life was leaving his body.

He raised his eyes, over which the film of death was stealing, and looked about the castle; the crystal crumbled off and split from top to bottom.

"Sacred powers!" prayed he, "forgive her as I forgive

her, and love her till the End, as I shall and for ever. Let her find what she seeks; let her wanderings once come to an end; let her soar through the air, if she must, till she comes to the purest sphere...." This sphere was the earth, the sweet Present, the little resting-point on which she could not wander, and thus felt within her the irresistible desire....

"Sacred powers, let her one day find what her happiness is. Then, if it is not I.... Let her find...."

His voice failed, his eyes opened as in a vision, and he whispered and finished his prayer: "... find ... in the Future!..."

That sacred word was his last. He died.

In the Kingdom of the Present, that once had been as a smiling garden, everything was now dead....

Then ... in the mist, which hung over the ridge of the mountains, something seemed to be creeping near, something with feet that could only move slowly. From many sides, over the hill-top, the strange creeping came nearer.... Gigantic hairy feet of monstrous spiders were walking over it; they came nearer and nearer; they were spiders with big, swollen bodies and feet always in motion....

They were the sacred spiders of Emeralda, Princess of the Past. Eagerly they ran to the dead garden of the Present....

They surrounded the garden and threw out their filaments to the crystal roof of the palace. Then they wove over the Present, that lay dead, one single gigantic web. . . .

And whilst they wove, the dead Present went to dust.

XVII

IN THE WOOD, in the autumn sun, Autumn was keeping festival.

The foliage shone resplendent in yellow, bronze, purple, golden-red, and pink; the sulphur-coloured moss looked like antique velvet. With gusts of wind, the branches, madly arrogant, shook off their exuberance of sere and yellow leaves, as if they were strewing the paths with silver and gold and rustling notes.

Loudly laughing danced the dryads through the whirling leaves.

Out of the foaming stream between moss-covered rocks, rose the white, naked nymphs.

"Where is she? Where is she?" cried the dryads inquisitively.

"There she comes! There she comes!" shouted the mad dryads, and in handfuls they cast the leaves into the air, which whirled over the nymphs and fell down on the water.

The dryads danced past, and the nymphs looked out inquisitively. They stood, a naked group, in their rocky bath; their arms were clasped round one another; green was their hair and white as pearls were their bosoms. The sere and yellow leaves kept whirling about. Trampling feet were approaching and were heard amongst the rustling leaves. Merry-makers were drawing near; the golden foliage quivered like a curtain of thin, fine, gold lace. . . .

"There she comes! There she comes!" exclaimed the nymphs with joy.

The branches cracked, the leaves whirled about, the tender sprays recoiled from the noisy merry-makers, who were advancing.

Nearer they came with the sound of pipe and cymbal. Drunken Bacchantes danced before them, waving the thyrsus, hand in hand with fauns and satyrs; they encircled a triumphal chariot, drawn by spotted lynxes.

High on the chariot sat a youth, beardless, with a wreath of vine-leaves round his forehead, full of laughter and animal spirits, with blue eyes that showed his love of pleasure. Naked were his godlike limbs, chubbily formed like the tender flesh of a boy, and his legs were long and slender, his arms rounded like those of a woman. He was the prince of the wood, of divine origin: Prince Bacchus was his name.

And next to him on the triumphal chariot, sat little Psyche enthroned. She too was naked, with nothing on but her veil, and her wings were so strikingly beautiful, crimson and soft yellow and with four peacock's-feather eyes. Round the chariot, close together as a bunch of grapes, sported madly a number of wine-gods, tumbling over one another, grape-drunken children.

In triumph the procession rushed on through the golden wood. The Bacchantes and satyrs sang and danced; two satyrs drove the lynxes, which, spiteful as cats, spat at them; the wine-gods entwined the vine and bore great heavy bunches of grapes.

High up, like a butterfly, which was a goddess, sat Psyche, and laughed with glistening eyes and glowing cheeks, waving to the nymphs.

"Live! long live Psyche—Psyche with the splendid wings!" shouted the nymphs.

The wind blew, the leaves whirled about; the procession swept past as though hurried along by the gale. A little wine-god had fallen and lay in the yellow leaves, playing with his chubby legs, purple-red from the juice of grapes; he was crying because he had been left behind; then he succeeded in getting on to his feet, and tottered after the procession. . . .

The nymphs laughed loudly at the little wine-god; they dived under and beneath the rocks.

The wind blew, the yellow leaves whirled about.

And the wood became still and lonely.

XVIII

"PSYCHE, STAY!" said Bacchus entreatingly.

"No, no let me alone!"

"With you goes all joy from the feast; Psyche, stay!"

"I will not always sing, dance, drink. No, no, let me alone!"

She pushed him away from her; she pushed the satyrs away from her; she broke the round dance of the Bacchantes, who, drunken, shouted with drunken eyes and wide-open screaming mouths.

"Psyche! Psyche!" screamed all.

She laughed loudly and coquettishly, like a spoilt child.

"I will come back tomorrow, when you are sober!" she said with a mocking laugh. "Your voices are hoarse, your song is out of tune, your last grapes were sour. I will only have the sweet of your feast, and the bitter I will leave to you. Spread out your panther skins; go and sleep off your drunkenness. If your feast has to last till winter, you need rest—rest for your hoarse throats, rest for your drunken legs, rest for your heads, muddled with wine. . . . I will come back tomorrow, when you are sober!"

She gave a loud, mocking laugh, and rushed into the wood. It was a moonlight night; in the pale moonbeams she left the wild feast behind. The jealous Bacchantes danced round Bacchus, and embraced him.

Psyche hastened on. Her temples throbbed, her heart beat, and her bosom heaved. When she was far enough away, she stopped, pressed both her hands to her bosom, and gave a deep sigh. More slowly she went on to the stream. Fresh was the autumn night, but burning were her naked limbs!

The wood was still, save that in the top-most branches the wind moaned. Like a silvery ship the moon sailed forth from the luminous, ethereal sea, and the rushing mountain-stream foamed like snow on the rocks. With a longing desire for coolness and water, Psyche stepped down to the flags on the bank; with her hands she put aside the irises, and made her way through the ferns and plunged her foot into the water.

Then the nymphs dived up.

"Psyche! Psyche!" cried they joyously, "Psyche with the splendid wings!"

Psyche smiled. She threw herself into the water, and the snow-white foam dashed up.

"Let me be with you a moment," entreated Psyche. "Let me cool myself in your stream."

The nymphs pressed round her and carried her on their arms. She lay down at full length.

"Cool my forehead, cool my cheeks, cool my heart!" she cried imploringly. "Dear nymphs, oh, cool my soul! Everything burns on me and in me; fire scorches my lips, fire scorches my brain.... O dear nymphs, cool me!"

The nymphs sprinkled water on her; Psyche put her arm round the neck of one of them.

"Your water-drops hiss on my forehead as on burning metal. Your flakes of foam evaporate on the fire in my breast. And on my soul, O dear nymphs, you cannot sprinkle your coolness!"

The nymphs filled their stream-urns and poured them over Psyche.

"Pour them all out! Put them all out!" cried Psyche entreatingly. "But although my hair is dripping, and my wings and my limbs too, my lips are scorched, my poor forehead burns, and within me, O nymphs, within me, my soul is consumed as in hell-fire!..."

'The nymphs took her gently in their arms; they dived with her below, they came up again; they kept diving up and down.

"Oh, bathe me, bathe me!" cried Psyche imploringly. "Benevolent nymphs, bathe me! Some coolness still hangs about my body ... but my soul, oh, my soul you can never cool!" She wept, and the nymphs caught up her tears in mother-of-pearl shells.

"Are you collecting my tears? Oh, no, they are not worth it. Once I wept a brook full; once they were drunk, drunk by Love; once they were pearls, and Love crowned me with them! Now, now they are like drops of wine, drops of fire, and though they should congeal and become rubies or topazes, they may never crown me more. Henceforth my tears, I shall always shed ... for Emeralda!"

In the shells the nymphs saw glistening pearls, and they understood not.... But all their urns they poured out upon Psyche's eyes.

"My eyes are getting cool, O beloved nymphs; many tears I shall never shed again; never again shall I weep a brook full.... But cool my soul, extinguish deep within me the burning flames!"

"We cannot, Psyche...."

"No, no, you cannot, O nymphs! Let me lie still then, still in your arms. Let me rock quietly to and fro on your white-foaming water, then let me sleep quietly.... But in my sleep my soul keeps burning; in my dreams I see it flame up, high up as out of a hole in hell.... Oh!"

She uttered a cry, as of pain.... The nymphs rocked her in their entwined arms, as in a cradle of lilies, and softly sang a song....

"Nymphs, nymphs!... This is the fire that nothing can extinguish—no, never.... This is remorse....

The nymphs understood her not; they rocked her and sang in a low, soft voice.

XIX

THAT MORNING she wandered about in the rosy autumn dawn—a mist between the trees stripped of leaves. Along the path she trod; on a skin she found a satyr and a Bacchante lying in a drunken sleep, tight in each other's arms; a cup lay on the ground, a broken thyrsus, pressed-out grapes. She hastened on and sought the most lonely spots. The foliage became scantier, the trees grew farther apart, the wood ended in a plain and, misty violet, a perspective of very low hills.

Psyche walked on over the plain and climbed the hills.

The autumn wind blew and howled between shrubs and bushes, and sang the approach of winter. But Psyche felt not the cold, for her naked limbs glowed: her soul was all on fire.

On the highest hill-top she looked out, her hand above her eyes, gazing into the violet mist. Unconscious to herself, she hoped for something vague and impossible: that she might see Eros, that he would come to her, that she would fall at his feet, that her would forgive her tenderly, and take her away with him.

Impossible. "What was impossible? Could not everything be possible? Had he not followed the track of her tears? Had he not found her in the arms of the Sphinx?" Oh, she hoped, she hoped, she hoped more definitely. Her remorse-burned soul longed for the balsam of his love in the palace of crystal, for the sounds of his lyre, for the tender words in the garden of the Present.

She hoped, she gazed. . . .

In the pale glow of the morning sun, the violet mist cleared up, and parted like violet curtains. . . .

She gazed: there was the Present. . . .

There Eros would be, mourning for his naughty Psyche!

There he would presently forgive her. . . .

Oh, how she hoped, how she longed! . . . She longed; she stretched out her arms and dared cry in a plaintive voice:

"Eros!"

The wind blew through bush and shrub and sang the approach of winter. The violet curtains of mist were drawn aside. The sad autumn morning appeared. There, now visible, lay the Present. . . .

And Psyche gazed, screening her eyes with her hand. . . .

There she saw her happiness of days gone by, destroyed. In a dead, withered garden, a ruin: crystal pillars crumbling to pieces. And between the pillars, spiders' webs; all over the garden spiders' webs, web upon web, and in them spiders with bloated bodies and lazy-moving feet. . . .

Then she saw that Emeralda was reigning!

Then she felt that Eros was dead!

She had murdered him!

Oh, how her limbs glowed, how her soul burned! Oh, the burning pain within her, deep within—a pain which no grape-juice could allay, which no mad dance could deaden and the nymphs could not cool, though they poured over her all their urns! Oh, that hell in her soul, for the irretrievable desolation, for the murdered one, past recall! Oh, that suffering, not for herself, but for him—for another! that repentance, that burning remorse!. . .

She fell to the ground and sobbed.

The pale sunbeams faded away, thick grey clouds came sweeping along, a shower of hail rattled down, flinging handfuls of icy-cold stones. . . .

She felt a touch on her shoulder. She looked up.

It was the Satyr who had allured her with his pipe, there, on that very spot.

"Psyche!" said he, "what are you doing here, so far away from all of us? Winter is coming, Psyche; listen to the whistling winds, feel the rattling hail; the last leaves are being blown away. We are going to the South, and

Prince Bacchus is searching for you.... What are you doing here, and why are you crouching down and weeping?"

"We are having a feast and are fleeing the winter; come!"

"I feel no cold; I am burning.... Let me stay here, and weep, and die...."

"Why should you die, O Psyche, Psyche, so pretty and so gay—Psyche, the prettiest and gayest, who can dance the maddest, who can dance out all the Bacchantes? Come!..."

She laughed through her tears, a laugh like a piercing shriek.

"But Psyche, do you know what it is?" said the Satyr, whispering confidentially. "Do you know what it is that prevents you from being happy, and why you are not like all of us? I told you before, Psyche: it is because of your wings. Your wings prevent you from butting a beast's skin round you, and entwining your hair with vine. The nymphs find your wings pretty, but what do you want with things that are pretty, yet of no use whatever? If you could only fly with those wings!"

"If I could only fly with those wings!" said Psyche, sighing. "No, I have never been able to fly with them, my poor, weak wings!"

"The nymphs think your wings pretty, but the nymphs are sentimental. The Bacchantes think them ugly, and laugh at you in secret. Prince Bacchus does not like wings either; he cannot embrace you well with those things on your back. Psyche, dear Psyche, listen: shall I tell you something?... You must let me cut off those wings with a pair of grape-scissors. For when you have got rid of your wings, then you can throw a panther's skin round you, and put a vine-wreath round your hair, and you will be altogether one of us...."

The wind blew, the hail rattled down: winter was coming on.

"Eros is dead!" murmured Psyche, "Spring is past, the Kingdom of the Present is withered, Emeralda reigns.... "What are you doing with things that are pretty, and have no use at all?...

"If I cannot possibly get cool, if I keep burning deep within me ... it is better, perhaps, to renounce my princess's rights, to go naked no longer, to have no wings...."

"Tell me, Psyche, may I cut them off?"

"Yes, clip them! Cut them right off, my wings, which are only pretty!" she cried fiercely. "Cut them off!"

His eyes glowed jet and gold, his breath came quickly from joy. He produced his sharp scissors....

And whilst she knelt, he cut off both her wings.

They fell on the ground and shrivelled up.

"Oh, that hurts, that hurts!... Oh, that hurts!" cried Psyche.

"It is a little wound, it will soon heal," said the Satyr soothingly, but grinning with pleasure.

Then he threw a panther's skin round her, put a wreath of vine-leaves on her head, and she was like a fair Bacchante still very young and tender, with her white skin, with her tender eyes of soulful-innocence, in which, deep down, dejection reigned.

"Psyche!" cried he delighted, "Psyche! How pretty you are!"

She uttered her shrill laugh, her laugh of bitter irony. He led her away down the hills. She looked about: yonder lay the Kingdom of the Present, reduced to dust and spider-webs. She looked about: in the wind, which was blowing, her wings whirled away, shrivelled up, whirled away like dry leaves.

She laughed and put her arm round his neck, and they hastened back to the wood.

The wind blew; the first snowflakes fell.

XX

SLOWLY FOLLOWED THE SEASONS—winter, spring, summer, autumn....

Winter, spring, summer, autumn, were the Present for a moment, and sank into the Past.

And again it was spring....

On the grassy plains, the shepherds drove out their flocks, and sang because the sky was blue, the world trilled with hope, in the new and tempered sunshine.

What did the shepherds know of Emeralda? They had never seen her. They sang, they sang; they filled the air with their song. As a reed, their song remained quivering and hanging in the air. In the wood and in the air, Echo sang with them their song. They sang because the sky was blue....

Emeralda they did not know....

Blue, blue ... blue was the air! Hope quivered in the sunshine, and love in their hearts....

Into the grassy plains the shepherds drove their flocks, and they sang because the sky was blue.

On the border of the wood, where endless plains extended, there lived in a grotto between rocks, a holy hermit who was a hundred years old.

How many seasons had he seen sink into the pits of the Past!...

How many times had he heard the Lenten song of the shepherds! Wrapped in contemplation, he heard them singing. They sang because the world trilled with hope.... They sang because fleecy lambs were sporting again in the meadows. They sang because they were young and loved the shepherdesses. They sang of blue sky, of hope, of lambs, and love....

The hermit continued deep in thought....

Every spring it was the same song, and he had never sung with them. Never had he known the Present, the spring Present of the shepherds.

The hermit continued deep in thought; he dreamed that Satan was tempting him, but his pious mind resisted. He dreamed that he had died in prayer, and his soul, purified, ascended into heaven.

Far off in the grassy plains was heard the bleating of the lambs, the voices of the shepherds.

The hermit heard a step. He looked up.

He saw a little form, as of a naked girl with no covering but her hair. And he thought it was really Satan, and he muttered an exorcism; he knit his brow, he crossed his arms.

The little form approached and knelt down.

"Holy father!" said she, in a low, trembling voice, "don't drive me away. I am poor and unhappy. I am a sinner, and come to you for help. I am not shameless, holy father, and I am ashamed that I appear before you naked. I asked the shepherdesses for something to cover me, but they laughed at me, drove me away and threw stones at me. Father, O father, men are merciless, they all drive me away.... I come from the wood, and wild beasts are not so cruel as men. In the wood the beasts spared me. A lion licked the wounds on my feet, and a tigress let me rest in the lair of her whelps. Holy father, the wild beasts had pity!"

"Then why don't you remain in the wood, devil, she-devil?"

"Because I must fulfil a duty among men."

"In my dream, soft voices have spoken to me, the voice of my father, and of him whom I loved, and they said: "Go among men, do penance...." But naked I cannot go among men, for they throw stones at me. And therefore, O father, I come to you, and entreat you: give me something to cover me! I have only my hair to hide me, and under my hair I am naked. O father, give me something to cover me! O father, give me your oldest mantle for my penance garb!"

The hermit looked up at her, as she knelt in her fair hair, and he saw that she was weeping. Her tears were blood-red rubies.

"He who weeps rubies has committed great sin; he who weeps rubies has a soul crimson with sin!"

The penitent sobbed and bowed her head to the ground.

"Here," said the hermit sternly, but compassionately. "Here is a mantle. Here is a cord for your loins. And here is a mat to sleep on. And here is bread, here is the water-pitcher. Eat, drink, cover yourself, and rest."

"Thanks, holy father. But I am not tired, I am not hungry and thirsty. I am only naked, and I thank you for your mantle and your cord."

She put on the mantle as a penance-garb, and whilst, red with shame, she covered herself, the hermit saw on her shoulder-blades two blood-red scar-stripes.

"Are you wounded?"

"I was, long ago...."

"Your eyes glow: have you a fever?"

"I do not know men's fever, but my soul is always burning like a cave in hell."

"Who are you?"

"One heavy burdened with sin."

"What is your name?"

"I have no name now, holy father.... Oh! ask no more.... And let me go."

"Whither are you going?"

"Far, along the way of thistles, to the royal castle. To the Princess Emeralda."

"She is proud."

"She is the Princess of the Jewel, and I weep jewels.

I shed them for her. Once there was a time ... that I wept pearls. ... O father, let me go!"

"Go, then. ... And so penance."

"Thanks, father. ... Oh, give me your blessing!"

The hermit blessed her. She went then as a pilgrim in her penance-garb. The path was steep and covered with thistles.

In the distance was heard the song of the shepherds.

XXI

THE PATH WAS STEEP, and covered with cactus and thistles. It was a narrow path, hewn out of the rocks, winding up the basalt mountain, where, high on the top stood the castle. The castle had three hundred towers, which rose to the sky; along them swept the clouds. In the path were many steps hewn out of stone.

Heavy masses of cactus grew on the side of the precipice, and over the leaves, prickly and round, Psyche saw the grassy valleys of the Kingdom of the Past, the villages, the towns, the river: a broad silver streak, and there, behind it, opal-like views, lakes in the sky, and quivering lines of ether. Higher and higher she went up the steps, up the path, in the gloomy, chilly shadow, whilst the sun shone over the meadows. She climbed up, and below she saw the shepherds with their sheep, and their song, quite faint, came up to her.

In the coppice she broke a strong stick for a staff. A lappet of her mantle she had drawn over her head as a hood. And with her staff and her hood, she looked like a pious pilgrim.

The solitary countryman who was coming down the rocky path, did not throw stones at her, but greeted her reverently.

She kept climbing up.

High in the air lay the castle, gloomy and inaccessible, a town of towers, a Babel of pinnacles; along it swept the clouds. As an innocent child, as a naked princess with wings, Psyche had lived there like a butterfly on a rock, had wandered along the dreadful parapets, had longed and hoped and dreamed. Oh! her longings of innocence, her hope to fly through the air to the opal islands, her dreams, pure as the doves that flew round about her!...

She had wandered through clouds, through desert and wood from the North to the South. She had loved the Chimera, had put questions to the Sphinx; she had been Queen of the Present and the beloved of Bacchus, and now ... now she came back, wingless, with a soul that burned her continually, like a scarlet child of hell; now she came back up the steep path....

Her penance-garb she had borrowed. But the thistles tore her feet, and pale from pain and suffering, from wounded feet, and ever-smarting shoulders, and a soul that burned continually, was her face, that peeped out from under her wide hood.

Up, up, she went, supporting herself with her staff....

Oh, the voice of her father, of Eros, in her dream, when the grape-dance was over! Then repentance had begun. Then she had fled through the wood, through the wild beasts. And the lion had licked her feet, and the tigress had allowed her to rest in the warm lair of her whelps. . . .

Then she went on, climbing higher and higher. . . .

Would she never get to the top? Would the castle, the Babel of pinnacles, the town of towers remain ever inaccessibly high in the clouds?

Her step left blood behind on the rocky stone.

But she did not rest. Rest did not help her.

She preferred to go on, to climb. If she walked, if she climbed, the sooner would she reach the castle.

Step by step she advanced. Oh, she was no longer afraid of Emeralda! What could Emeralda do to her to make her afraid? What greater suffering could her sister inflict upon her than the pain of remorse, that was ever with her wherever she went!

And on she climbed, and the thistles tore her feet, and the solitary man who was coming down the rocky path greeted her reverently, when he saw the blood of her footstep.

XXII

THE NIGHT was pitch dark, when she stood before the awful gate and asked admittance.

And the guards let her in because she wore a holy dress. The halberdiers took her to the hall, where they slept or kept watch, and invited her to rest.

Psyche sat down on a rude bench, she ate their brown soldier's bread and she drank a drop of their wine.

Then she offered them a ruby for their hospitality and evening meal.

And while they wondered that a pilgrim possessed such a beautiful jewel, she said in her strange voice, weak, tired, and yet commanding:

"I have still more topazes and rubies and dark purple carbuncles. Tell the princess that I have come to do her homage and give her my jewels."

The message was sent to Emeralda, and the queen asked the pilgrim to come. She sent pages to conduct her to the throne where she sat.

And Psyche understood that Emeralda was afraid of treachery, afraid of the approach of soul, and therefore was so surrounded by armed men.

She passed between the pages, up the steps, over passages; then iron gates were opened, and a curtain was drawn aside.

And Psyche stepped into the golden hall of the tower. There sat Emeralda in the light of a thousand candles, on a throne, under a canopy, surrounded by a great retinue.

"Holy pilgrim!" said Emeralda, "be welcome! You have come to bring me jewels?"

A cold shiver ran like a serpent over Psyche's limbs, when she heard Emeralda's voice. She had not thought that she would be afraid any more of her proud sister, but now when she saw her and heard her voice, she almost fainted from fear.

For her look was most terrible.

Emeralda had grown older, but she was still beautiful. Yet her beauty was horrible. In the hall, lit up with thousands of candles, a hall of gold and enamel, sat Emeralda like an idol on her throne of agate, in a niche of jasper. There was nothing more human about her; she was like a great jewel. She had become petrified, as it were, into a jewel. Her face, that was ivory white, like chalcedony; from her crown of beryl there hung down her face six red plaits of hair, as inflexible as gold-wire, and stiffly interwoven with emeralds. Her mouth was a split ruby, her teeth glittered like brilliants. Her voice sounded harsh and creaking, like the noise of a machine. Her hands and inflexible fingers, stiff with wings, were opal-white, with blue veins such as run through the opal. Her bosom, opal, chalcedonic, was enclosed in a bodice of violet amethyst— and over the bodice she wore a tunic of precious stones. Her dress was no longer brocade, but composed of jewels. All the arabesque was jewels; her mantle was jewelled so stiffly that the stuff could not bend, but hung straight down from her shoulders like a long jewelled clock.

And she was beautiful, but beautiful as a monster, preciously beautiful as a work of art—made by one, both jeweller and artist, barbarously beautiful, in the incrustations of her crown, the facets of her eyes, the lapis lazuli of her stiffly folded under-garments, and all the gems and cameos which bordered her mantle and dress.

In the light of thousands of candles she glistened, a barbarous idol, and shot forth rays like a rainbow, representing every colour; dazzling, fear-inspiring was her look, pitiless and soulless.

Proud she sat and motionless, glistening with lustre, oppressed by the weight of her splendour; and covetous, her grating voice said again eagerly:

"Holy pilgrim, welcome! You have come to bring me jewels?"

Psyche gained courage.

"Yes," she said in a firm voice. "Powerful Majesty of the Past, I come to do you homage and bring you jewels. But I beg that we may be left alone."

Emeralda hesitated; but when Psyche remained silent, her cupidity got the better of her fear and she gave a sign. She raised her stiff hand. And by that single movement she cracked and creaked with grating jewels, and shot forth rays like the sun, which, like a nimbus, streamed around her. Her retinue disappeared through side-doors. The shield-bearers withdrew. Psyche stood alone before her sister. And then Psyche unfastened the cord round her waist and took off her mantle; her long hair fell about her, and she was naked. Naked she stood before Emeralda, and said:

"Emeralda, don't you recognise me? I am Psyche, your sister!"

A cry escaped the princess. She rose up; she creaked; her splendour and pomp grated, and she glittered so, that Psyche was dazzled.

"Wretched Psyche!" she exclaimed. "Yes, I know you! I have always hated you, hated as I hate everything that is gentle, I hate doves, children, flowers! So you have deceived me, intruder! You bring me no jewels!"

Psyche knelt down and showed her open hand.

"Emeralda, I offer you the homage which I once refused you. I present you with topazes, rubies, and dark purple carbuncles. I kneel in humility before you.

134

I offer you my tears, which have turned into stone, and I ask you humbly: punish me and give me a penance to do. Look! I have lost my wings. I may not go naked any longer. I have committed sin. Emeralda, make me do penance! Inflict on me the heaviest that you can think of. If I can do it, I will do it. Lay a heavy task upon my wingless shoulders."

Emeralda looked down at kneeling Psyche. The princess approached her sister, took the jewels, examined them attentively, held them up to the light of the candles, and then dropped them into an open casket. Thoughtfully she continued gazing at Psyche. And she seemed to Psyche like a gigantic jewel-spider, watching from the midst of her glittering web the rays of her own splendour. But whatever she were, princess, sun, spider, or jewel, a woman she was not, a human being she was not, and through the opal of her bosom gleamed her heart of ruby.

Psyche, kneeling penitent, spoke not, awaiting her fate, and Emeralda watched her.

Thoughts, mechanical as wheels, rolled through her brain. She thought as a machine. She was inexorable, because she had no feeling; she thought inhumanly because she had no soul. Soulless she was and hard as stone, but she was powerful, the mightiest ruler of the world. She ruled with a movement, she condemned with a look, she could kill with a smile; if she spoke a word, it was terrible; if she appeared in public there was disaster; and if she rode through her kingdom in a triumphal chariot, then everything was scorched by her lustre and crushed under her triumph.

At last she spoke, motionless like a spider in her web of glittering rays, and her voice sounded like an oracle in a screeching incantation.

"Psyche, fled from her father's house, fallen from all princely dignity, dethroned Princess of the Present, immoral Bacchante, corrupt and wingless, weeping tears of scarlet sin—listen!

"Psyche, who wandered frivolously to purple streaks of sky, who longed for the nothingness of azure and of light, who loved a horse, who forsook her husband, who wandered and sought and asked, in desert and in wood—wander, seek, and ask!

"Wander, seek, and ask, till you find!

"Wander along the flaming caves, seek in the fire-vomiting mouths of monsters, ask of the martyred spirits, who roll upon the inky sea.

"Descend to the Nether-world! Seek the Mystic Jewel, the Philosopher's Stone that gives the highest omnipotence; seek the Mystic Jewel, the rays of which reach to eternity and penetrate to the Godhead.

"Descend, wander, ask, seek, and find!"

Her voice grew terrible, and, screeching, she stepped nearer, and with a look at the casket, said pitilessly:

"Or ... weep for it ... suffer for it. I care not how much."

She paused, and then in a voice of horrible hypocrisy, continued:

"And then, if you bring me the Sacred Jewel, the name of which may not be uttered...." She drew still nearer.

"Then be blessed, Psyche, and share with me, Emeralda, your sister, the divine omnipotence!"

Like an oracle sounded her hypocritical voice. She felt in Psyche an unknown power; she feared for her soul, and wished to gain that power for herself, to make sure of the two-fold omnipotence of the world, both soul and body. And in the horrible penance which she laid upon Psyche, she feigned tender love. Creaking and cracking, she drew nearer, and in her web of rays shed a sunbeam over her kneeling sister, and with her stiff opal fingers stroked the bent head with its fair, long tresses.

An ice-cold shiver ran through Psyche, as if her burning soul were being frozen.

"I obey," she murmured.

And she rose up, intoxicated from splendour, stiff from icy coldness. She tottered and shut her eyes. When she opened them, she was in a gloomy ante-chamber, clad in her coarse mantle; and the shield-bearers approached with torches.

"Conduct me to Astra!" she commanded.

There was something strange in her voice which made them obey, the voice of a princess, the soft voice of command, which appealed strangely to the men, as if they had heard it when they were pages.

They conducted Psyche through halls, over passages, up steps, to another tower. They opened low doors, and, through silent vaults, guided the strange pilgrim, rich in rubies.

"Who comes there?" asked a voice, tired, weak, and faint.

Then the men left Psyche alone, and she was with Astra, and she saw her sister in the twilight on the terrace, sitting before her telescope, surrounded by globes and rolls of heavy parchment spread out. And Psyche saw Astra, looking very old, with thin grey hair, which hung down her wax-white face, from which two dull eyes stared out; her white dress hung down limp on her sunken shoulders, her withered breast and attenuated limbs. Bitter dejection was in her dull eyes; her thin hand hung down powerless, tired, and incapable of work, and her voice, faint and weak, said:

"Who comes there?"

"I, Psyche, your little sister, come back, O Astra, as a penitent!..."

"As a penitent?"

"Yes, I fled, committed sin, and now I will do penance...."

Astra mused.

"It is true," she murmured. "I remember, little Psyche. Come nearer. Take my hand, I cannot see you."

"The night is dark, Astra. there are few Stars in the sky, and the torches are not yet lit...."

"No? Is it dark about me? That does not matter, Psyche, for I cannot see, I am blind...."

Psyche gave a cry.

"Astra! Poor sister, are you blind? Oh! you who could see so well! are you blind?"

"Yes, I have gazed myself blind! I have turned my telescope from left to right, to all the points of the universe. I thought to become the centre, the kernel of science, the focus of brilliant knowledge; now I am blind, now I see nothing more, now I know nothing more. The colossal numbers have become confused in my brain since the living Star on my head faded. Do you still see its faint splendour between my grey hair? Ah! now I have your hand.

"What is that, child? What round things are falling over my fingers?"

"My tears, Astra, poor Astra!"

"How hard they are and cold! What hard, cold tears, Psyche!... Sit down here at my feet. Is the night dark?

139

Are the torches not yet lit? Well, let it be dark, for I see nothing; but I feel you, I feel you hair; now stroke your head, round and small. I feel along your shoulders, Psyche, little child with wings.... But your wings I do not feel.... Have you none now? Have they been cut off? My star has faded, and your wings are cut; Emeralda triumphs alone! Her gift from the fairy has brought her prosperity. Her heart of ruby feels no pain; she is clad in the majesty of precious jewels. She is hard and beautiful, hard as a stone, beautiful as a jewel.... Psyche, creep close to me.... We can do nothing against her, child. My star is faded, your wings clipped; we have lost our noble rights.... I am old, but you—are you still young? You feel so young, indestructibly young.... You have suffered so, asked and wandered ... not appreciated your happiness, and murdered Eros! Poor child, you a murderess!... You weep rubies ... You will do penance. You are strong, Psyche, and always young.... You will do penance after all your sins! Emeralda has laid penance on you.... To seek the Philosopher's Stone in the caverns of flaming hell! O Psyche, the Stone does not exist. The unutterable name is a legend. The Jewel exists only in the pride of man. The universe is limited, the Godhead is not limited; no rays from precious stones can reach the Godhead and rule over God. No looking through lenses of diamond can penetrate the

Godhead. It is all pride and vanity. Psyche, there is nothing but resignation. Emeralda is powerful, but more powerful she cannot become....

"In vain will you seek."

"Yet I will seek, Astra, although it be in vain.... And do you also, sister, lay penance on me..., Let me do penance for Astra, as I do for Emeralda."

"No, child, I know no penance. There is nothing but resignation. There is nothing but to wait. Everything else is vanity and pride. But do penance, little Psyche. Penance is illusion, yet illusion is pleasant: illusion ennobles. Believe, poor child, in your penance, believe in your illusion. I have never known it. I have always calculated. The colossal numbers roll through my dull and hazy brain in endless series of figures. However you count, you never come to the sum of the endless.... The stars cannot be counted. The farthest sun is incomputable, the divine is limitless. Even the nearest frontier of the Future is beyond computation. There is a sea of unfathomable light.... O Psyche, I am tired, I am blind, and I shall soon die. In this place, here I will stay. Psyche, look through the telescope. Is the night too dark? Do you see anything?"

"The stars give a dim light."

"Look through the telescope. What do you see? Tell me, what do you see?"

"In the glass, right at the top, I see a dark spot, which emits a few rays. Is that a black star?"

"No, Psyche, that is a spider. Emeralda has sent a spider. The spider has crawled to the top, along the smooth diamond; there the spider weaves his web. And the diamond ... is crumbling to pieces...."

"Astra!..."

"Psyche, creep closer to me.... Let me feel your little round head, your wingless shoulders...."

"Astra, everything is black; clouds are drifting past the stars!"

"Sleep thus in my mantle, sleep thus at my feet. Sleep, my little child, and cover yourself for the night.... Psyche, your old nurse is dead. Psyche, now I am your nurse.... Sleep now by blind Astra...."

Feeling for Psyche, she threw her mantle round her. The night was dark. Astra's powerless hand dropped over Psyche. Psyche fell asleep.

XXIII

IT WAS STILL DARK when Psyche awoke. She looked up at Astra, who sat sleeping, her grey head on her breast; faintly shone her star. Very gently, so as not to wake her, Psyche rose, and left the terrace. She knew the way. She went through the halls and passages, down the steps, the endless steps. In the corners sat the sacred spiders, and wove....

Psyche went lower down, to the vaults. There burnt the everlasting lamps. She went among the royal tombs, crystal sarcophagi, and found her father's coffin. By the lamp, which was always kept burning, she recognised his embalmed, rigid face. The eyes were closed. He knew nothing about her: that she had gone away and come back. Death was between them, and severed them forever.

She kissed the glass, and her tears, round, hard, and red, clattered on the crystal.

She knelt down and tried to pray. In a corner of the vault, a black spot moved. It was a big spider with a white cross on its body.

"So, you have come back again.... I knew that you would come. We can escape from nothing. Everything

143

happens as it happens. Everything is as it is. Everything goes to dust; into the pits of the Past, into the power of Emeralda.... Now become a spider like us, weave your web, and be wise...."

Psyche got up.

"No!..." she exclaimed, "I will not become a spider, I will weave no web. I have sinned, but I will weave no web; I have sinned and will do penance. The world is awful—desert and wood and space; life is awful— love and pain, joy and despair, sin and punishment. And if fate is as it is, it is in vain to weave a web and to heap up treasures of dust. Spider, were it not more human to love, to live, and even to sin, than to weave web upon web? Spider, I envy you not your sacredness!...

The spider puffed itself out maliciously.

"You seem to be still proud of your murder and your immorality and shamelessness! Your princely name you have dragged through the mire, your wings you have given up for a panther's skin and a grape-wreath, and know not yet what repentance is. If you had been wise and had become a spider, you would have served Emeralda, and there would have been no need to go down to the Underworld!"

But Psyche was no longer afraid. She had come to kiss her father's coffin; she left her jewelled tears in the treasure, which the spiders watched over, and ascended the hundreds of steps and came on to the terrace of the battlements.

There as a child she had wandered and gazed, a child with wings, and innocent, her soul full of dreams. Now she wandered again along the ramparts and battlements high as a man; the doves fluttered about her, the swans looked up at her ... and full of dejection for former innocence and youth, she wept and wept: no longer a brook, but topazes, rubies, tears of sin, that, rattling down, frightened the doves and the swans, which, indignant, thought that she was pelting them with stones. The doves flew away, and the swans, offended, turned their backs on her. Then she sat down in an embrasure—no wings now lay against the stone-work—and she folded her arms round her knees. She looked towards the horizon; behind it loomed other horizons, first pink, then silver; blue, then gold; behind the grey, pale and misty, and then fading away. Then beyond, the horizon became milk-white, like an opal, and in the reflection of the last rays of the setting sun, it seemed as if lakes were mirrored there; islands rose in the air, aerial paradises, watery streaks of blue sea, oceans of ether and light-quivering nothingness.

And Psyche bowed her head, full of sadness, and sobbed. The world was not changed, but more beautiful than ever; gloriously beautiful loomed the ever-changing horizon. Yet Psyche sobbed, full of sadness. She knew that the horizons were pure delusions, and that behind them was the desert with the Sphinx. Oh! if she could once more believe in the aerial paradises, the purple seas, the golden regions with people of light, who lived under rosy bananas! Alas! had she not trod a paradise, the sweet Present, the adorable garden of a moment, so little and so short in duration? It was past, it was past! Oh, how her soul scorched, how her shoulders ached, how her eyes burned!

She wept and she sobbed, and hid her face in her hands. She did not notice that the wind was rising, that the horizon quivered, that clouds were speeding through the air, white colossi like towers and dragons, riders and horses.

She did not see the changes in the sky; she did not see the going up and down of wings, of flaming wings in the silver lightning that flashed from the sky; she did not hear the warning thunder, not did she see the clouds emitting sparks. But suddenly she distinctly heard a voice:

"Psyche! Psyche!"

She looked up. Before her, she saw descending on broad wings a steed of pure light and flame. And she uttered a cry, that sounded in the air like an endless shout of gladness:

"Chimera!"

It was he. He descended. The basalt terrace trembled, as though shaken by an earthquake; under his hoofs the stone shot sparks, and he stood before her resplendent and beautiful.

"Chimera!" she cried, and folded her hands and sank down before him on her knees.

She could say nothing else. She was dazzled, and it seemed as though her soul ascended heavenward in the pure delight of love.

"Psyche!" sounded his voice of bronze, "I have come down, for I love you. But I may not bear you any more on my back through the delusive regions of air, because you have committed sin. Psyche, it is your bounden duty to obey Emeralda's command. Go down to Hell and seek the Jewel."

"Chimera, adored one, delight of my soul, oh, your splendour fills my eyes! Your word gives strength to my weakness! I feel it! You may not bear me away; I am unworthy of your wings. But I adore and bless you for coming! Chimera, Chimera, your splendour has beamed once more upon me! your voice has inspired me, and I will do what you say. You let the light of hope break in upon me; new strength flows through my limbs. Chimera, I hope, I hope! I will go down into Hell; I will seek. . . . Shall I find? I know not. . . . But I hope! The horizon, is quivering with hope and ether and the Future!

"Psyche!" sounded his voice again like bronze, "be strong? Take heart! Descend! Do penance! Seek! Once more you will see me?"

"Once more!"

"Be strong, take heart, do penance!"

He ascended, whilst Psyche remained kneeling. When he was high in the air, there came a peal of thunder, as if the heavens would burst asunder. The sky was dark, but lit it up by the lightning. In the black sky, in the lightning flame, rose fearfully the three hundred towers. And the thunder-claps rumbled on, one after the other, as if the Past were perishing in the last day....

With a joyful cry, Psyche hastened along the terraces, the battlements, ramparts, entered the castle, and went down the steps. Lower and lower she descended, lower than the vaults; and as she passed them, she threw a kiss in the direction where the old king lay buried.... She descended still lower, and yet she heard the thunder pealing above, and the castle seemed to tremble to its very foundations.

She descended still lower: she descended very deep pits, built like towers reversed to the central nave of the earth. She descended step after step, thousands of steps, groping in the darkness. She walked with unerring feet, that felt for the next step, that detected the slippery stone; she felt and never hesitated. Another step and then another; again a pit, pit after pit, all the pits of the Past. Bats flew up and flapped their wings, spiders she felt crawling over her, an icy dampness fell like a chill wind upon her shoulders.

Deeper down she went, and deeper. It was pitch dark, and above she heard nothing more; she heard only the flapping of gigantic bats, the droning of the envious spiders. But she defended herself with her little hand; as she descended, she beat about her, beat the bats away, seized a vampire, held it tightly by the neck, and strangled it.

Her foot glided over toads, she slipped over snakes, but she got up again and beat the bats and fought with the vampires. The Chimera had so inspired her with strength, that she felt strong as a giant, young and courageous; he had filled her eyes with such light that she saw him in the darkness.

In the pitchy darkness his flaming wings were distinctly visible. And on she went descending; thick clouds of dust, the deepest shadows of Emeralda's transitoriness, rose up, but she kept breathing, never hesitating, and her foot felt instinctively the next step, and she struck at the bats and fought with the vampires. When she throttled them, a human cry was heard, and the echo sounded a thousand times like the anxious cry of a murder. But she was not afraid. She kept on descending. . . .

She kept descending. At last she felt no more steps but a void, under her feet, and she sank ... like a feather, through heavier air; she sank, she sank deeper and deeper, deeper and deeper.... A black draught of air, an invisible wind, damp and chill, made her feel that she had passed all the pits, that she was sinking outside them in the open air, invisible and black, thick as ink. Then she began to sink more slowly, and ... her feet touched the ground. Sounds soft and low, like the plaintive strains of a viol, rose up from afar, like music of the sea, the plaint of a thousand voices which never became melody.

The far-off sound continued quivering as an accompaniment of wind, of a black wind which blew, and overpowered, the music of the sea. Sometimes it went a little higher, sometimes a little lower, and always remained the vague and distant incomprehensible harmony.

From where the wind came, from where the plaintive murmuring arose, thither would Psyche go. And with her foot she kept feeling, and with her outstretched hands, on and on she went....

Long, long she went in the darkness, till the darkness became less opaque and lit up with phosphoric flickerings; and she saw:

That she was ascending a path between two inky seas. Black as ink were the waves.

Then she heard them roaring; then she saw their crests lit up with a blue phosphorescent glow.

Then she heard the soft, low sounds, the plaintive viols swell, till they became a dull, and continuous soughing.

The black wind rose as with a gigantic sail, and suddenly blew the hurricane.

In the pitch-dark air, the lightning flashed blue.

And between the two inky seas, Psyche went slowly on, against the gusts of wind.

Then she uttered a cry, as though she were calling.

The hurricane took her cry for help over the endless sea of Hell. . . . And from all sides dived up the gruesome frights—leviathan monsters. They opened their jaws at Psyche, and the water streamed out. Their scaly tortuous bodies wound along over the black surface of the ocean, and on the horizon, they dived up and down, and the ocean dived with them. Storm-flood, waterfall—storm-flood, waterfall. . . . They spread out their dragon wings, and caught up the boisterous wind; they shot up waterspouts like towering fountains, of a blue and yellowish hue. Their round squinting eyes stood out watchful, like green and yellow signals; they lifted their red-lobed jaws, abysses of red-slimy desires, bubbling with foamy slaver.

"Monsters of the sea of pain, where shall I find the Jewel for Emeralda?"

Psyche asked the question in a high, musical key, and her voice rang out clearly in the hurricane and plaintive moanings of the sea. Her high soprano sounded above all the roaring of the elements and plaintive cries; and three times she repeated the question:

"Monsters of the sea of pain, where shall I find the Jewel of Emeralda?"

The leviathans pressed together along the path that Psyche trod. But amidst the noise of their tossing and snorting and spouting, she heard the plaintive sea swelling, the sea of plaintive voices; and then in the blue phosphorescent glow between the monsters, she saw the drowned shades heaving to and fro, always writhing in fear, always drowning in the inky sea; the everlasting wailing of the plaintive sea, the cry of souls in pain; the gigantic plaintive viol, with strings ever playing. . . .

"Vanity, vanity!"

Did she hear aright?

It was one single sound, like a note repeated again and again. "Vanity, vanity!" was the inexorable answer, first vague as a dream, mystic as a thought, sounding more distinctly as an admonition against worldly pride. And so distinct did the sound become, that Psyche, brave Psyche, who feared neither vampire nor monster of the deep ... that courageous Psyche hesitated and felt all her strength giving way.

"If it were vanity to seek, to ask for the Jewel, how much farther should she go?"

"Should she go back?"

She looked round.

But she saw that behind her step, the seas immediately closed till they became one single sea of ink; she saw that the only path for her stretched across the seas, that behind her it immediately sank away.

She could not go back, she must go on.

And she buoyed up her sinking soul; she went on, and in a high soprano voice repeated again and again her question:

"Spirits in the sea of pain, where shall I find the Jewel for Emeralda?"

"Vanity, vanity!"

The plaintive viol kept trembling, and the same sound sounded ever, the unchangeable answer. The hurricane was no longer chill, but warm, sultry, strangely sultry; more and more sultry blew the everlasting cyclone.

The sea-monsters kept back; they dived again below; the sea sank with them, the shadows swayed to and fro in storm-flood, waterfall—storm-flood, waterfall, and many-headed hydras came sinuously up. The sea no longer shone with phosphorescent glow, but was quite black, pitch black, black as boiling pitch, without foam and without light, and kept sending up a discharge of miry, vaporous matter. In the boiling pitch, the hydras, with their thousand snaky heads, kept diving up, tortoise-scaled; swayed to and fro, to and fro the pale faces of the shades, but ever sounded the plaintive viol, and ever rang forth the same note, the unchangeable answer to Psyche's shrill question:

"Hydras of the sea of pain, spirits in the sea of pain, where shall I find the Jewel for Emeralda?"

"Vanity, vanity!..."

The pitch seethed and hissed and steamed.

It was no longer a sea of water, no longer a sea of pitch;

It was a sea of nothing but flame, pitch-black flame, a sea of jet-black fire, fire and flame, that waved from the horizon, where a single streak of pale light appeared. In the black flames burned the shades, in the black flames wound the hydras in and out; the thick smoke shot up into the clouds, and the clouds sent it back again....

"Spirits in the pitch-black flames, where shall I find the Jewel for Emeralda?"

"Vanity, vanity!..."

The hurricane kept blowing, the plaintive viol kept trembling, and ever sounded the same note, the unchangeable answer. But scorchingly, more scorchingly blew the wind, like a tempest from a sun for ever doomed. The black night now assumed a dark-purple steam; the clouds drove a bloody vapour into the heavens.

And on either side of Psyche's path suddenly shot out the flaming hurricane of the sun, gigantic purple tongues of fire, scarlet and orange. The lower clouds drove them back, and when Psyche looked round, she stood in a flaming fire. The flaming hurricane seethed round her; behind her feet the path was on fire. The air was fire. But Psyche, whose own soul was on fire, in her own scorching fire of remorse, felt not the glowing heat, and she saw,

Out of the living scarlet craters, the orange caves, the hellish chimeras working up their sinuous way like glowing spirals: half arabesque, half beast; half dragon, half tail; flaming sea-horses. They spat and fanned the glowing fire, and, riding aloft on the burning hurricane, the shades swept past Psyche.

"Spirits in the scarlet flames...."

"Vanity, vanity!"

This was the only answer, that sounded afar off in her ears, the answer of the tortured, angry spirits, which in the strength of their sin and passion came flying up from the craters.

On she went....

She went on along the path that unfolded before her.

How confidently she went on, how calmly! Why was she not afraid? Oh! she knew too much to be afraid and not to go on in confidence. Was the answer not always more distinct and unchangeable? Psyche's soul breathed freely, and in the fire around her her own fire seemed to diminish. For when the fire round her became yellower, sulphur-yellow, pure yellow, the pure golden yellow of the sun, then she uttered a cry of joy, as though she knew the answer:

"Spirits in the sulphur flames, spirits in the sun's flames!..."

She smiled.... Smiling, she hastened on with joyful voice, with winged step; and so rapidly did she flee along the path smoothed out for her tread, that behind her the answer could scarcely reach her.

"Vanity, vanity!"

Oh! it was always the plaintive viol, but the too poignant grief was tempered with melancholy; the plaintive sea became like a sea of melancholy; the thousands of voices were full of melancholy. And when the flames became less dense and lighter, when they changed from sulphur yellow to soft azure, a flaming sea of azure, in the silent dawning moonlight scenery, high broad, blue flaming tongues that shot from the moon—when the hellish hurricane no longer raged, but gave way to a more benign breeze then Psyche asked no more in so shrill a key, but knowing all, her voice murmured dejectedly:

"Spirits in the azure flames, where shall I find the Jewel for Emeralda?"

The melancholy viol vibrated more gently; the spirits rocking to and fro in the thin blue fire sang more softly:

"That is vanity, Psyche; that is vanity...."

She uttered her jubilant cry, and hastened on with uplifted arms through the azure moonflames. The firmament spread out in higher circles and formed wider spheres;

The flames became clearer and clearer; more benignly blew the breeze;

And pale, the spirits flitted to and fro: pale shades with melancholy eyes, singing their song of painful remembrances....

And the spirits looked at Psyche—the spirits smiled benignly on her, astonished that she was still alive.

They pointed for her to go on farther and farther; they nodded to her, "On! on!"

And she gave a loud cry of joy and hastened on....

She sped through the flames and shades;

Till the flames were still, and high and white;

High, still, white flames, like sacrificial flames, like altar flames, high in the sky, the lofty sky, the wide sky; the wide expanse full of white flame—still, white, ascending, purifying flames, refined and clear, over the whole wide expanse, the wide refining expanse.

Once more she asked the pale shades, who swarmed about between the flames, hand in hand, who swayed continually to and fro between the flames:

"Spirits in the white flames, pure white, in the white flames, where shall I find the Jewel for Emeralda?"

"Vanity, vanity!" sang the shades softly and quietly, and in the answer, calm and assuring, of the expectant penitents, vibrated the great viol with a sound like a soft jubilant trill.

Psyche asked no more. She slackened her speed and began to walk, her arms raised, her head erect, through the silvery flames. Oh, the dear, tender flames, the adorable purifying flames! how they cooled, in their snow-white glow, the burning remorse of her soul!

How freely Psyche breathed, in the innocently white glowing fire! Like lilies were the tongues of flame, fragrant and soothing as balsam, cool and fresh as snow ... cold as water, as foam. The white flames foamed and rippled like a sea, lower and smoother, quieter and more serene; they rippled like a sea of lilies, like a sea of silver snow.... They became moisture and water and foaming ocean, the tender element of gentle compulsion, carrying along as an irresistible dream, white as paradise, and as slightly rippling waves of foam, they bore Psyche away.

On the foaming waves Psyche drifted along, all white in the golden boat of her fair hair. So gently did they rock her, the foaming, rippling waves, that Psyche shut her eyes. Sleep was stealing over her. Her lips smiled with inward peace.

The waves bore her away, the sea washed her ashore. She awoke from her slumber; pearl-white she rose from the foam, amidst the joyful dolphins.

She stepped out of the sea on to the land. She felt quite cool, and her soul was calm and peaceful, full of reassuring, holy knowledge. But within her was a great desire.

Smiling, she stretched out her arms. She yearned for the desire of her heart....

"Not yet ... not yet," was whispered tenderly to her cool and peaceful soul. "Wait, wait ..." sounded the echo.

In the silent joy of her soul, she wept. She lifted her hand to her eyes; wet were her tears, and in her hand ... lay a pear!...

Then she looked round. She recognised the sea-shore with its many bays, the shore of the Kingdom of the Past. There, on the pool-blue horizon, loomed a town of minarets and pinnacles, of cupolas and obelisks, surrounded with golden walls.

That was the capital of the kingdom. Thither she would repair.

There, proud and peaceful, still and cool, she would say to Emeralda, her powerful sister,

That her Jewel was vanity. That the gem did not exist.

XXIV

W HEN PSYCHE approached the capital, she heard at the gates the excited cries of festive merry-makers. Outside the gates flocked the noisy crowd, dressed in all the colours of the rainbow, and bedecked with flowers, singing and dancing, but not knowing why. Everywhere was bustle and commotion; on the roadside sat hundreds of hucksters, and women extolling their wares—glasses with jewels and fruit, cooling drinks, dresses and flowers. In a shrill key they praised their wares; they spread out their stuffs with much ado, and offered the people flowers, and poured them out wine, and held up strings of glass pearls and cheap necklaces of coins.

Psyche was naked, and she veiled herself in her hair; she spread over the marks on her shoulders her gold-en mantle of hair, and as many of the dancing girls, some half naked and others quite naked, danced round, hand in hand, people thought that she was naked, only because she was so fair—Psyche, so pearl-white in her golden hair. She was not wont to be ashamed of nakedness, which was once her right, her privilege as a princess; but now under the eyes of the people she blushed, and walked with downcast eyes. Then she turned to a saleswoman and asked:

"What is the feast for?"

"Where do you come from? 'What is the feast for!' Don't you know anything about it?"

"I come from the other side of the sea...."

"What is the feast for!' It is the great Festival, the Jubilee-festival, of Emeralda. It is the Triumphal Procession of the Queen!"

"It is the Triumphal Procession of the Queen!" resounded on all sides. They danced and sang:

"It is the Triumphal Procession of the Queen!"

They were drunk with joy, dizzy from strange joy; but Psyche suddenly saw that they were deadly pale and frightened, deadly pale under paint and flowers, and frightened whilst they danced round in a ring.

"I have no dress for the occasion; give me that veil of golden gauze!" said Psyche to the saleswoman.

"That is very dear!"

"I will pay you for it with this pearl."

"With that pearl! Are you a princess, then!"

Psyche then took the veil and she bound it round her loins, just as she used to do before.

"I will give you a wreath of fresh roses as well!" said the woman, pleased, and put the flowers on her head.

She smiled, and it suddenly occurred to her that she was decked out with those flowers as a victim for the altar; that all the people who were making merry and dancing were bedecked as victims. She went on. Through the round gold gate she entered the city; the squares were seen in the distance, connected with very broad streets; square palaces of marble and bronze, of jasper and malachite, round cupolas and finely pointed minarets, glistened in the sun as if conjured up by magic. They stretched far away, and right behind the blue mountains rose the royal castle, a Babel of pinnacles and towers innumerable, almost indiscernible in the distance, with square ramparts and walls, and lofty summits lost in the rising mist. And along the squares, over palaces, and on the minarets, hung the thick festoons of flowers, as though the towns were decked out for an offering. Close up to the castle, Babel of pinnacles, the festoons of flowers seemed to reach. And in the squares the dancers threw flowers into the air, and it seemed as if white roses were raining down from heaven. To the sound of tabour and cymbals, the people danced madly round, and ever was heard the same cry:

"It is the Triumphal Procession of the Queen!"

Then Psyche, in the secret depths of her heart, saw clearly and indubitably what it all meant. As she went along with the dense crowds of noisy, shouting merrymakers, she saw all the people in the town trembling with fear, which made the blood congeal in their veins.

Their eyes, through fear, were ready to start out of their sockets; their teeth chattered; their limbs, bedecked with flowers, trembled; the sun was shining, but everyone was shivering with cold.

But no one spoke of his trembling, and they danced, madly drunk with foolish joy, and they kept shouting the same thing:

"It is the Triumphal Procession of the Queen!"

XXV

A GREAT COMMOTION was going on in the direction of the castle. In that direction all eyes were turned, and the dancing girls forgot to dance. From fear, the crowd stood still, as if petrified, and forgot to conceal the anxiety of their minds. The palaces seemed to tremble; the air quivered audibly. Something dreadful was about to happen.

The royal castle shone with a strange lustre; a sun seemed to send forth a halo; an ominous aureola appeared in the distance. The fearful rays of the Sun of Consternation outshone the day, outshone the sun: from their centre, they penetrated through houses and people.

And everything shone, softened by the glow of piercing sunbeams. The rays quivered everywhere in the air, and the aureola filled the world.

The cause of consternation came rattling on with the rapidity of an arrow.

All hearts stood still, all breath was taken away, all dancing was stopped, all rejoicing ceased.

From the castle, over the triumphal wall a triumphal chariot rattled along with the speed of an arrow. On the top, a living jewel, stood Emeralda, and guided the four and twenty steeds. It was her splendour and her aureola which appeared in the air. It was her rays which caused the houses to shine with splendour and pierced the people with flashes. She stood immovable, clad in the strength of precious stones, in a tunic of sapphires, in a robe of brilliants, with deep flounces of gems and white cameos; her mantle was like a bell, with folds of purple carbuncle, lined with enamelled ermine. From her crown of beryl, from her heart of ruby, the rays shot forth, shone out her fear-inspiring aureola and streamed over the town and in the air, eclipsing the sun, which turned pale. Her eyes of emerald, stars in her opal face, chalcedonic, looked inexorable and her bosom of precious stones heaved not. Only her heart of ruby beat regularly, and then her lustre grew alternately dim and bright. . . .

She stood immovable and guided her horses, her four-and-twenty foaming stallions, rearing greys, which drew her triumphal chariot, like a broad enamelled shell on innumerable wheels, on cutting wheels so numerous, that they seemed to run into one another— a turning confusion of spokes.

The dazzling, fear-inspiring chariot rattled on with the rapidity of an arrow. And suddenly, awaking from their stupefaction, the people madly danced again and shouted the same jubilant cry. The tabours sounded, the white roses rained down, and before the queen the people prostrated themselves and paved her path with their bodies. The grey stallions foamed and reared; they came on, they came on, they trampled over the first bodies—men and women, girls and children, dressed for a festival and bedecked with flowers. . . . Over her people rode Emeralda; the innumerable wheels rattled, a confusion of spokes, revolving, cutting furrows in flesh and blood, reducing blood and human flesh to a muddy mass. But farther up they danced, farther up they sang, before casting themselves down for her Triumph. . . .

Then Emeralda, looking over her triumphal way, saw with the keen glance of her black carbuncle pupil, a little form, naked and fair, who lifted up her small child's hand.

And fiercer and fiercer gleamed her heart of ruby, for she had recognised the form.

And the desire flamed up in her: the thirst for more power and to become like a god.

Emeralda recognised Psyche. And she reined in her twelve pairs of horses, she drove them more slowly, and under the less quickly revolving wheels she heard the jubilant cry of the dying people. The blood dropped from the wheels, but the roses rained down and covered the horrible sight. On the bloody, muddy mass, the roses rained down, white, from the balconies of the palaces.

Emeralda stopped.

Under her, death was silent.

Around, the town was silent. She alone reigned and shot out her terrible fan of rays, which scorched the houses and pierced the air.

And before her, at a little distance, stood Psyche, proud, pearl-white, crowned with roses, in a veil of gold.

And the silent crowd recognised in her the third princess of the kingdom.

"Psyche!" said Emeralda, and her voice sounded loud through the town from the focus of her rays, "have you come to bring me the unutterable Jewel, the Gem of Power, the Bestower of Universal Power, the sacred Stone of Mysticism? Have you found the Mystery of the Godhead, and,

"—Do you rule with me the Universe and God?"

The town shuddered and quivered. The people were stupefied.

The surrounding air trembled audibly.

Then Psyche's voice sounded clearly, limpidly, from the consciousness of the wisdom and sacred knowledge which she possessed.

"Emeralda, for you I have gone through Hell along the black seas, oceans of pitch, along the horrible sloughs of flaming hurricanes, along the craters and caverns scarlet and yellow, along the azure fires and through the white and lilac glow. Give heed to what I say. Hell answered 'Vanity!'; the chimeras hissed 'Vanity!'; the spirits cried 'Vanity!'; and the whole plaintive viol trilled:

'*Vanity!*'

"Do you understand me, Emeralda? Your wish was Vanity, for the mystic Jewel that bestows godlike power is Vanity, and ... *Does not Exist.*"

Then it was terrible. The queen, a living idol, burned with rage, blazed with rage; her heart was inflamed with rage.

Around her, decked out for sacrifice, in festive garb, in the sunshine and her own dazzling splendour, her people trembled with fear. And cruelty gleamed in her fixed face; her emerald eyes started so revengefully from their sockets as though blinded by their own splendour, and she pulled at the numerous reins....

The horses reared, the white roses fell down, the people screamed with joy and the fear of death, and the triumphal chariot rattled on.

Swift as an arrow it thundered on over the people, who paved the way in ecstacy, and Psyche saw the maddened horses approaching, snorting, foaming, panting, trampling, pulling, their eyes round and mad....

For a moment she stood firm, proud, tall, pearl-white in the sacred knowledge she possessed; then the angry hoofs struck her down, and the horses trampled her as a flower. Emeralda's chariot rattled over her, with its many cutting wheels, and whilst she died like a crushed lily, trampled in her own lily-whiteness, she thought of her old father, and how she had crept to his breast and hidden her face in his beard, before she went to sleep at night. . . .

She died. . . . But while she lay trampled to death in the mud of human flesh and blood, and the sacrificial roses kept falling down over her corpse unrecognisable.

She returned to life, hovering through the air, and felt so light and unencumbered, and was whiter than ever and naked.

And on her tender shoulders she felt two new wings quivering!. . .

She hovered over her own body into a drifting cloud, a mist of fragrance, which farther on she lost sight of; and light, white, and rarefied, she looked wonderingly at her trampled body and laughed. Strange, clear, and childlike sounded her laugh in the cloud and vapoury fragrance. . . .

XXVI

THE TRIUMPHAL CHARIOT rattled on madly. Emeralda stretched out her sceptre, on the top of which glowed a star of destroying rays. When she stretched out the sceptre and directed the rays, she scorched monuments, palaces, and parks to a white ash, and, for her cruel jubilant procession, she cut down everything that came her way. The thick white ashes flew up like dust; the jubilant multitude were scorched; the palaces of jasper and malachite shrivelled up like burnt paper; the breath of the horses blew away, like ash, the white burnt gardens. And right over everything went Emeralda, scorching as she went. Powerful, foolish, arrogant, and proud she was, and more unfeeling than ever, spiteful and cruel, hurt in her pride; and she scorched, and made the way smooth before her. Behind her lay all the town, and she drove through her kingdom, filling the air with her rays. She drove through valleys and burnt up the harvest; she reduced villages to dust; she dried up rivers; and before her, the mountains split asunder.

Her sceptre made a way for her, and no law of nature resisted her power. The air was grey with the clouds of ash which rained down upon the earth.

She went along as swiftly as an arrow, swiftly as light, swiftly as thought. She went so swiftly, that in a single hour she had gone all round her wide kingdom intoxicated with the pride of annihilation, and she drove her maddened horses through endless plains of sand.

Desert after desert she consumed; the lions fled before her; she overtook them in a moment; clouds of sand she sent up into the air. . . .

But then she relaxed her speed. She stopped.

Before her, grey and high through the clouds of sand and falling ash, there loomed a most dreadful shadow.

The shadow was like a gigantic beast, squatting in the sand, with a woman's head in a stiff basalt veil. The woman's head had a woman's breast, two basalt breasts of a gigantic woman. But the body that squatted in the sand was a lion, and the paws stuck out like walls. And so great was the shadow, so monstrous the beast, that even the triumphal chariot of Emeralda appeared small.

"Sphinx!" said Emeralda, "I will know. I am powerful, but there is power above me. There are spheres above mine, and there are gods above my divinity. There are laws of nature which my sceptre cannot alter. Sphinx, tell me the riddle. Reveal to me the place where the Jewel lies hidden, which gives almighty power over the world and God, so that I may find it and become the mightiest of all gods. Sphinx, answer me, I say! Open your stony lips and let your voice once more be heard, that shall make the world tremble with wonder. For centuries you have not spoken. Sphinx, speak now! For if you do not speak, Sphinx, and reveal to me where the Jewel lies hidden, then great and terrible as you are, I will scorch you to a white ash and go over you in triumph. Sphinx, speak!"

The Sphinx was silent. The Sphinx looked with stony eyes at the clouds of sand and raining ash. Her basalt lips remained shut.

"Sphinx, speak!" said Emeralda, threateningly and red with rage.

The Sphinx spoke not and looked.

Emeralda stretched out her sceptre and directed the destroying rays.

The rays split on the basalt with crackling sparks like flashes of forked lightning. Emeralda uttered a cry, hoarse and terrible. She threw away her broken sceptre. But of her greater power she did not doubt, and for the last time she threatened.

"Terrible Sphinx, tremble! I am more terrible than you! Speak, Sphinx!"

The Sphinx was silent.

Then Emeralda tugged at her reins.

The maddened horses reared, snorting, foaming, panting, trampling, pulling, and dashed against the Sphinx.

But the foremost horses were dashed to pieces against the god-like basalt.

Then Emeralda uttered cry after cry, one hoarse cry after another, which resounded through the desert. She tugged at the reins; the horses, despairing of their attack against the immovable, drove at the Sphinx, and fell back crushed, falling over one another and trampling one another to death; the triumphal chariot split, and the splinters of sparkling jewels flew up like cracking fireworks, and Emeralda fell between the still revolving wheels. And her heart of ruby broke. All her dazzling splendour suddenly faded. The terrifying fan-like aureola suddenly grew dim, and the desert was grey and gloomy, with a gentle rain of thick white ash falling down.

The Sphinx was silent, and looked on. . . .

XXVII

PSYCHE WAS ALIVE AGAIN, soaring through the air, and felt so light and ethereal; pearl-whiter she was than ever, and naked.

And on her tender shoulders she felt two new wings fluttering!...

She hovered away over her own dead body into a drifting cloud, a fragrant mist, which farther on she lost sight of; and light, white, and ethereal, she looked with wonder at her trampled corpse and laughed....

Strange, clear, and childlike sounded her laugh in the cloud and vapoury fragrance....

"Psyche!"

She heard her name, but so dazzled and astonished was she, that she did not see. Then the wind blew about her; the cloud moved, the fragrance ascended like incense, and she saw many like herself, restored to life, hovering in the fragrant cloud, and round her she distinguished the outlines of well-known faces.

"Psyche!"

She recognised the voice, deep bronze, but yet strange. And the wind blew about her and she saw a bright light before her, and recognised the Chimera!

"You promised me: once more!" exclaimed Psyche.

She threw herself on to his back, she clung to his mane, and he soared aloft.

"Where am I?" said Psyche. "Who am I? What has happened? And what is going on around me? Am I dead, or do I live? Chimera, how rarefied is the air! How high you ascend! Are you going to ascend higher, higher still? Why is everything so dazzlingly bright about us? Is that water, or air, or light? What strange element is this? Who are going up with us—ethereal faces, ethereal forms? And what is the viol that is playing?

"I heard that once before. Then it sounded plaintively; now it has a joyous sound!

"Chimera, why is the air so full of joy here?... Look! below us is the Kingdom of the Past.

"It lies in a little circle, and the castle is a black dot. Chimera, where are you going so high? We have never been so high before. Chimera, what are those circles all round us, the splendour of which makes me giddy? Are those spheres? Do they get wider and wider? Oh, how wide they get, Chimera, how wide! How high it is here, how wide, how rarefied and how light is the air! I feel myself also so light, so ethereal! I feel myself also so light, so ethereal! Am I dead?... Chimera, look! I have two new wings, and I shine pearl-white all over. Do I not shine like a light? It is true I have been very sinful. But I was what I had to be! Is it good to be what

we have to be? I do not know, Chimera: I have
thought of neither good nor bad; I was only what I
was. But tell me, who am I now, and what am I? And
where are you taking me so quietly, so safely; up and
down go your wings, up and down. The stars are twin-
kling round us; around us whirl the spheres, and wider
and wider they become!... How light, how ethereal!
What is that I see on the horizon? Or is it not the horizon? Opal islands, aerial oceans.... O Chimera! I see
purple sands wrinkling far, far away, and round them
foams a golden sea.... We saw that once before, but
not as it is now! For then it was delusion, and now!...
The sands are growing more distinct; I see the ripple
of the golden sea.... Chimera! What land is that? Is
that the rainbow? Is that the land of happiness, and are
you the king?"

"No, Psyche, I am not a king, and that Land...."

"—And that Land?..."

"Is .... the Kingdom of the Future!"

"The Future! the Future! O Chimera, where are you
taking me to? Will the Future not prove to be a delusion?..."

"No, here is the Future. Here is the Land. Look at it
well... well...."

"It is wider than the widest sphere, wider than anything I can think of. Where are the limits?"

"Nowhere."

"How far and how wide is the widest sphere?"

"Immeasurably far, indescribably wide...."

"And what stretches away round the widest sphere?"

"The unutterable, and the *All, All!* The...."

"The?..."

"I know no names! On earth things are called by names; here not...."

"Chimera!... On the purple strand I see a town of light, palaces of light, gates of light.... Do beings of light dwell there?... Are these the fore-spheres of the farthest sphere?... Is that the way through circles to the Chimera? I see forms, I see the people of light! O Chimera! I know them! That is my father, and that.... O joy, O joy!... that is Eros! Eros! Quicker, Chimera—annihilate the space which separates us; speed on, ply your wings faster—away, away! Oh, faster, Chimera! Can you not go faster? You fly too slowly for me! You fly too slowly! I can fly faster than you."

She spread out her tender, light, butterfly wings; she rose above the breathless, winged horse, and ... she flew!... She glided over the Chimera's head toward the strand, toward the city, toward the blessed spirits. There she saw her father, there she saw Eros—Eros, godlike and naked, with shining wings!

Round her the viol of joy played its joyous notes, as if all the spheres rejoiced. In the divine light, the faces of the cherubim began to blossom like winged roses.

She glided swiftly through the air to her father and Eros, and embraced them. She laughed when she saw the flaming Chimera approaching, because she could fly faster than he!

"Come!" cried Eros joyfully. And he wanted to take her to the gate, from whence sunbeams issued like a path of sunny gold: a path along which enraptured souls were going hand in hand. . . .

But the kingly shade stopped them for a moment, when they, Eros and Psyche, intoxicated with love, embraced each other. . . .

"Look!" said the shade. Look down below. . . ."

They saw the Kingdom of the Past, with their glorified minds, lying visible, deep in the funnel of the spheres. They saw the castle, fallen to ruins, with a single tower still standing. They saw Astra, old, grey, and blind, sitting before her telescope, gazing in vain. They saw her star flicker up for a moment with a bright and final light.

Then they saw Astra's blind eyes .... see! Astra looked and beheld the land of light, and the little band of happy, loving, dear ones in their shining raiment. Then they heard Astra murmur: "There! There . . . the Land!. . . The . . . Kingdom . . . of . . . the . . . Future!"

And they saw her star extinguish:
She fell back dead. . . .
The viol of gladness trilled.

Cupid and Psyche

Translated by
Robert Graves

I

ONCE UPON A TIME there lived a king and queen who had three very beautiful daughters. It was possible to find human words of praise for the elder two, but to express the breathtaking loveliness of the youngest, the like of which had never been seen before, was beyond all power of human speech. Every day thousands of her father's subjects came to gaze at her, foreigners too, and were so dumbfounded by the sight that they paid her the homage due to the Goddess Venus alone. They pressed their right thumbs and forefingers together, reverently raised them to their lips and blew kisses towards her. The news spread through neighbouring cities and countries that the goddess, born from the deep blue sea and nourished upon the froth of its foaming waves, had now come among the multitudes of mortal men and everyone was allowed to gaze at her; or else, that this time, the earth, not the sea, had been impregnated by a heavenly emanation and had borne a new Goddess of Love, all the more beautiful because she was still a virgin. The princess's fame was carried farther and farther to distant provinces and still more distant ones, and people made long pilgrimages over land and sea to witness the greatest wonder of their age. As a result, nobody took the trouble to visit Paphos or Cnidus or even Cythera to see the Goddess Venus. Her rites were put off, her temples allowed to fall into ruins, her sacred couches trodden underfoot, her festival neglected, her statues left ungarlanded and her altars left bare and unswept, besmirched with cold ashes.

Worship was accorded to the young woman instead and the mighty goddess was venerated in human form. When she went out on her morning walks, victims were offered in her honour, sacred feasts spread for her, flowers scattered in her path and rose garlands presented to her by an adoring crowd of suppliants who addressed her by all the titles that really belonged to the great goddess of Love herself. This extraordinary transfer of divine honours to a mortal greatly angered the true Venus. Unable to suppress her feelings, she shook her head menacingly and said to herself: "Really now, so I, all the world's lovely Venus whom the philosophers call 'the Universal Mother' and the original source of the elements, am expected to share my sovereignty, am I, with a mortal girl! And to watch my name, which is registered in heaven, being dragged though the dirty mud of Earth! Oh, yes, and I must be content, of course, with the reflected glory of worship paid to this girl, grateful for a share in the worship offered to her instead of to me—and allowing her, a mortal, to display her appearance as mine! It meant nothing, I suppose, when the shepherd Paris, whose just and honest verdict Jupiter himself confirmed, awarded me the prize of beauty over the heads of my two goddess rivals? No, I can't let this creature, whoever she may be, usurp my glory any longer. I'll very soon make her sorry about her good looks—they're against the rules."

She at once called her winged son Cupid, that very wicked boy, with neither manners nor respect for the decencies, who spends his time running from building to building all night long with his torch and his arrows, breaking up everyone's marriage. Somehow he never gets punished for all the harm he does, though he never seems to do anything good in compensation. Venus knew that he was naturally bent on mischief, but she tempted him to still worse behaviour by bringing him to the city where the princess lived—her name was Psyche—and telling him of her rival beauty. Groaning with indignation she said; "I implore you, as you love your mother, to use your sweetly wounding arrows and the honeyed flame of your torch. You'll give your mother revenge in full, most secretly, against the impudent beauty of that girl. You'll see that the princess falls desperately in love with some perfect outcast of a man—someone who has lost rank, fortune, everything;

someone who goes about in such complete degradation that nobody viler can be found in the whole world."

After she had uttered these words she kissed him long and tenderly and then went to the nearby sea-shore, where she ran along the tops of the waves as they danced foaming towards her. At the touch of her rosy feet the deep sea suddenly calmed, and she had no sooner willed her servants from the waters to appear, than up they bobbed as though she had shouted their names. The Nereids were there, singing in unison, and Portunus, with his bristling bluish beard, and Salacia, with her bosom filled with fishes, and the little Palaemon riding on a dolphin. After these came troops of Tritons swimming about in all directions, one blowing softly on his conch-shell, another protecting Venus from sunburn with a silken veil, a third holding a mirror before the eyes of his mistress, and a team of them yoked two and two, harnessed to her car. When Venus proceeds to the ocean she's attended by quite an army of retainers.

Meanwhile Psyche got no satisfaction at all from the honours paid her. Everyone stared at her, everyone praised her, but no commoner, no prince, no king even, dared to make love to her. All wondered at her beauty, but only as they might have wondered at an exquisite statue. Both her less beautiful elder sisters, whose reputation was not so great, had been courted by kings and successfully married to them, but Psyche remained single. She stayed at home feeling miserable and ill, and began to hate the beauty which everyone else adored.

The poor father of this unfortunate daughter feared that the gods and heavenly powers might be angry and hostile, so he went to the ancient oracle of Apollo at Miletus and, after the usual prayers and sacrifices, asked where he was to find a husband for his daughter whom nobody wanted to marry. Apollo, though an Ionian Greek, chose, for the sake of this teller of a Milesian tale, to deliver the following oracle in Latin verse:

> *On some high mountain's craggy summit place*
> *The virgin, decked for deadly nuptial rites,*
> *Nor hope a son-in-law of mortal birth*
> *But a dire mischief, viperous and fierce,*
> *Who flies through aether and with fire and sword*
> *Tires and debilitates all things that are,*
> *Terrific to the powers that reign on high.*
> *Great Jupiter himself fears this winged pest*
> *And streams and Stygian shades his power abhor.*

The king, who until now had been a happy man, came back from the oracle feeling thoroughly depressed and told his queen what an unfavourable answer he had got. They spent a number of days weeping, mourning and lamenting. But the time for the grim fulfilment of the cruel oracle was now upon them.

The hour came when a procession formed up for Psyche's dreadful wedding. The torches chosen were ones that burned low with a sooty, spluttering flame; instead of the happy wedding-march the flutes played a querulous Lydian lament; the marriage-chant ended with funereal howls, and the poor bride wiped the tears from her eyes with her flame-coloured veil. Everyone had turned out, groaning sympathetically at the calamity that had overtaken the royal house, and a day of public mourning was at once proclaimed. But there was no help for it: the divine commandment had to be obeyed. So when the ceremonies of this hateful wedding had been completed in deep grief, the entire city followed the tearful Psyche, a living corpse, in procession, escorting her not to her marriage but to her grave.

Her parents, overcome by grief and horror, tried to delay the dreadful proceedings, but Psyche exhorted them: "Why torment your unhappy old age by prolonging your misery? Why weary your hearts—which I claim as my own rather than yours—with continual lamentations? Why spoil the two faces that I love best in the world with pointless tears? Why bruise your eyes—which are mine as well? Why pull out your white hairs and beat your breasts, which I so deeply revere? Now, too late, you at last see the reward that my beauty has earned you; the deadly curse of hateful jealousy for the extravagant honours paid me. When the people all over the world celebrated me as the New Venus and offered me sacrifices, then was the time for you to grieve and weep as though I were already dead; I see now, I see it clearly, that the one cause of all my misery is this use of the goddess's name. So lead me up the rock as Fate has decreed. I am looking forward to my lucky bridal night and my marvellous husband. Why should I hesitate? Why should I shrink from him, even if he has been born for the destruction of the whole world?"

After uttering these words, she walked resolutely forward. The crowds followed her up to the rock at the top of the hill, where they left her. They returned to their homes with bowed heads, extinguishing the wedding-torches with their tears. Her broken-hearted parents shut themselves up in their palace and gave themselves up to unending darkness.

Psyche was left alone weeping and trembling at the very top of the hill, until a friendly air of the gently breathing West Wind sprang up. It gradually swelled out her clothes until it lifted her off the ground and carried her slowly down into a deep valley at the front of the hill, where she found herself gently laid out on a bed of the softest turf, starred with flowers.

And so Psyche, reclining comfortably in this soft and herbaceous place, upon a bed of dewy grass, began to feel rather more composed, and fell peacefully asleep. When she awoke, feeling thoroughly refreshed, she rose and walked calmly towards the great, tall trees of a nearby wood, through which a clear, crystalline stream was flowing. This stream led her to the heart of the wood where she came upon a royal palace, too wonderfully built to be the work of mortal man. You could see, as soon as you went in, that some god must be in residence at so pleasant and splendid a place.

The ceiling, exquisitely carved in citrus wood and ivory, was supported by golden columns; the walls were sheeted with silver on which figures of many kinds of beasts were embossed and seemed to be running towards you as you came in. To have created this masterpiece, with all those animals engraved in silver, was clearly the work of an exceptionally gifted man, or rather of some demi-god, or, truly, some god, and the pavement was a mosaic of all kinds of precious stones arranged to form pictures. How lucky, how very lucky anyone would be to have the chance of walking on a jewelled floor like that! And the other parts of the palace were just as beautiful and just as fabulously costly. The walls were faced with massive gold blocks which glittered so brightly with their own radiance that the house had a daylight of its own even when the sun refused to shine; every room and portico and doorway streamed with light and the other riches of the house were in keeping. Indeed, it seemed the sort of palace that Jupiter himself might have built as his earthly residence. Psyche was entranced. She went up to the entrance and after a time dared to cross the threshold. The beauty of what she saw lured her on; and every new sight added to her wonder and admiration. She came on splendid treasure chambers stuffed with unbelievable riches; every wonderful thing that anyone could possibly imagine was there. But what amazed her even more than the stupendous wealth of this treasure of ecumenical dimensions, was that no single chain, bar, lock or armed guard protected it.

As she stood gazing in rapt delight, a disembodied voice suddenly spoke: "Do these treasures astonish you, lady? They are all yours. Why not go to your bedroom now and rest your tired body. When you feel inclined for your bath, we, your maids, will be there to help you, and after you have refreshed yourself you will find a royal banquet ready for you."

Psyche was grateful to the unknown Providence that was taking such good care of her and did as the disembodied voice suggested. First she relieved her weariness by a sleep and a bath, then straight away she noticed a semi-circular table, all laid for dinner, just for her. She sat down happily—and at once nectarous wines and appetizing dishes appeared by magic, not brought in by anyone but floating up to her of their own accord. She saw nobody at all but only heard words uttered on every side; the waiters were mere voices, and when someone came in and sang and someone else accompanied him on the lyre, she once again saw nothing. Then the music of a whole invisible choir came to her ears and she seemed to be in its midst, though none of the singers were to be seen.

When these pleasures came to an end, and darkness called, Psyche went to bed; and at a late hour of the night she heard a gentle whispering near her. Being all alone, she feared for her virginity and trembled and quaked, and was all the more frightened by the prospect of something bad happening to her because she did not know what it might be. Then came her unknown husband and climbed into her bed, and made Psyche his wife.

He left her hastily before daybreak, and at once voices were heard in the bedroom comforting her for the loss of her virginity.

That is how things went on for quite a time until, as one might expect, the novelty of having invisible servants wore off and she settled down to what was a very enjoyable routine; despite her uncertain situation she could not feel lonely with so many voices about her.

Meanwhile, her father and mother, as they grew old together, did nothing but weep and lament, and the news of what had happened spread far and wide until both her sisters heard all the details. In grief and sorrow they left their homes and hurried back earnestly to see and speak to their parents.

On the night of their arrival Psyche's husband, whom she still knew only by touch and hearing and not by sight, warned her: "Lovely Psyche, darling wife, cruel fate menaces you with deadly danger. Guard against it vigilantly. Your elder sisters are alarmed at the report of your death. They will soon be visiting that same rock you came to, in order to see if they can find any trace of you. If you happen to hear them mourning for you up there, you must not answer them, nor even look up to them; for that would cause me great unhappiness and bring utter ruin on yourself."

Psyche promised to do as her husband asked; but when the darkness had vanished, and so had he, she spent the whole day in tears, complaining over and over again that not only was she a prisoner in this wonderful palace without a single human being to chat with, but her husband had now forbidden her to relieve the minds of her mourning sisters, or even to look a them. She spent the whole day weeping, and that night she went to bed without supper or bath or anything else to comfort her. Her husband came in earlier than usual, drew her to him, still weeping and expostulated with her: "O Psyche, what did you promise me? What may I—I who am your husband— expect you to do next? You have cried all day and all night, and even now when I hold you close to me, you go on crying. Very well, then, do as you like, follow your own disastrous fancies; but when you begin to wish you had listened to me, the harm will have been done."

She pleaded earnestly with him, swearing that she would die unless she were allowed to see her sisters and comfort them and have a talk with them. In the end he consented. He even said that she might give them as much gold and as many necklaces as she pleased; but he warned her with terrifying insistence not to be moved by her sisters' ruinous advice to try to discover what he looked like. If she did, her impious curiosity would mean the end of all her present happiness and she would never lie in his arms again.

She thanked him for his kindness and was quite herself again. "No, no," she protested, "I'd rather die a hundred times over than lose my lovely marriage with you. I love you, I adore you desperately, whoever you are; even Cupid himself can't compare with you. So please, I beg you, grant me one more favour! Tell your servant, the West Wind, to carry my sisters down here in the same way that he carried me." She kissed him coaxingly, whispered love-words in his ear, wound her limbs closely around him and called him: "My honey, my own husband, soul of my soul!". Overcome by the power of her love he was forced to yield, however reluctantly, and promised to give her what she asked, but he vanished again before daybreak.

II

MEANWHILE Psyche's sisters inquired their way to the rock where she had been abandoned. Hurrying there they wept and beat their breasts until the cliffs re-echoed. "Psyche! Psyche!" they screamed. The shrill cry reached the valley far below and Psyche ran out of her palace in feverish anxiety, crying: "Why are you mourning for me? There's no need for that at all, here am I, Psyche herself! Please, please stop that terrible noise and dry all those tears. In a moment you'll be able to embrace me, after all those lamentations for my fate."

Then she called up the West Wind and gave him her husband's orders. He at once obliged with one of his gentle puffs and wafted them safely down to her. The three sisters embraced and kissed rapturously. Soon they were shedding tears of joy, not of sorrow. "Come in now," said Psyche, "come in with me to see my new home and relieve your sorrows with your sister Psyche." Then she showed them her treasure chambers and let them hear the voices of the big retinue of invisible slaves. She ordered a wonderful bath for them and feasted them splendidly at her magical table. But after they had filled themselves with all these divine

delicacies they both felt miserably jealous—particular-
ly the younger one, who was very inquisitive. She never
stopped asking who owned all this fabulous wealth; and
she pressed Psyche to tell her who and what sort of a
man her husband was.

Psyche was loyal to the promise she had made her
husband and gave away nothing; but she made up a
story for the occasion. He was a handsome young man,
she said, a little downy beard just beginning to shadow
his cheeks, and spent his time hunting in the neighbouring hills and valleys. But then, fearing that all the
garrulity should make her contradict herself or cause
her to make a slip and thus give away her secret, she
loaded them both with goldwork and jewelled necklaces, then summoned the West Wind and asked him
to fetch them away at once. He carried them up to the
rock but on their way back to the city the poison of
envy began working again in these worthy sisters'
hearts, and they exchanged animated comments.

One of them said: "How blindly and cruelly and
unjustly Fortune has treated us! Do *you* think it fair that
we three sisters should be given such different des-
tinies? You and I are the two eldest, yet we get exiled
from our home and friends and married off to foreigners who treat us like slaves; while Psyche, the result
of Mother's last feeble effort at child-bearing, is given
all these riches and a god for a husband, and doesn't

even know how to make proper use of her tremendous wealth. Sister, did you ever see such masses of glittering jewels? Why, the very floors were made of gems set in solid gold! If her husband is really as good-looking as she says, she is quite the luckiest woman in the whole world. The chances are that as he grows even fonder of her he will make her a goddess. And, my goodness, wasn't she behaving as if she were one already, with her proud looks and condescending airs? She's only a woman after all, yet she orders the winds about and is waited upon by invisible attendants. Whereas it's my wretched fate that my husband's older than Father, balder than a pumpkin and more puny than a little boy; and he locks up everything in the house with bolts and chains."

"My husband," said the other sister, "is doubled up with sciatica, which prevents him from making love to me except on the rarest occasions, and his fingers are so crooked and knobbly with gout that I have to spend half my time massaging them. Look what a state my beautiful white hands are in from messing about with his stinking fomentations and disgusting salves and filthy plasters! I'm treated more like a surgeon's assistant than a wife. You're altogether too patient, my dear; in fact, to speak frankly, you're positively servile, the way you accept this state of affairs. Personally, I simply can't stand seeing her living in such undeserved style. Remember how haughtily she treated us, how she bragged of her wealth and how stingy with her presents she was. Then, the moment she got bored with our visit, she whistled up the wind and had us blown off the premises. But I'll be ashamed to call myself a woman, if I don't see that she gets toppled down from this lavish life she's leading. And if you feel as bitter as you ought to feel at the way she's insulted us both, what about joining forces and working out some plan for humbling her? Now, in the first place, I suggest that we show nobody, not even Father and Mother, these presents of hers, and let nobody know that she's still alive. It's bad enough to have seen her luck, and a lamentable sight it was, without having to bring the news home to our parents, and have it spread all over the place; and there's no pleasure in being rich unless people hear about it. Psyche must be made to realize that we're not her servants, but her elder sisters. We'll go back to our husbands and our shabby (but at least respectable) homes, and when we can finally think of an effective scheme let's see each other again here and humble her pride."

The two evil sisters approved of this evil plan. They hid the valuable presents that Psyche had given them and each began scratching her face and tearing out her hair in pretended grief at having found no trace of their sister; which made the king and queen sadder than ever. Then they separated; each went back full of malicious rage to her own home, thinking of ways of ruining her innocent sister, even if it meant killing her.

Meanwhile, Psyche's unseen husband gave her another warning. He asked her one night: "Do you realize that a storm is brewing? It will soon be on you and, unless you take the most careful precautions, it will sweep you away. These treacherous hags are scheming for your destruction; they will urge you to look at my face, though as I have often told you, once you see it, you lose me for ever. So if these hateful vampires, with their harmful designs, come to visit you again—and I know very well that they will—you must refuse to speak to them. Or, if this is too difficult for a girl as open-hearted and simple as yourself, you must at least take care not to answer any questions about your husband. For we have a family on the way: though you are still only a child, you will soon have a child of your own, which shall be born a god if you keep my secret, but a mortal if you divulge it."

Psyche was exultant when she heard that she might have a god for a baby, and proud of this fine pledge of her love that was on the way, and of her exalted status as a mother. She began excitedly counting the months and days that must pass before it was born. But having never been pregnant before she was surprised that her belly should swell so large from such a diminutive beginning.

The wicked sisters were now hurrying to Psyche's palace again, ruthless Furies breathing out the venom of snakes, and once more her husband, stopping briefly, gave her this warning: "Today is the fatal day. Your enemies are near. They have taken up their arms, struck camp, marshalled their forces and sounded the 'Charge'. They are enemies of your own sex and blood. They are your wicked sisters, rushing at you with drawn swords aimed at your throat. O darling Psyche, what dangers surround us! Have pity on yourself and on me. Keep my secret safe and so guard your husband and yourself and our unborn child from the destruction that threatens us. Refuse to see or hear those wicked women. They have forfeited the right to be called your sisters because of the deadly hate they bear you, which has shattered the blood-tie; they will come like Sirens and lean over the cliff, and make the rocks echo with their murderous voices."

When she heard this Psyche, her voice broken with sobs, said: "Surely you can trust me? You have long since had convincing proof of my loyalty and my power of keeping a secret; and in the future you will once again approve of my steadfast behaviour. Only tell the West Wind to do his duty as before, and allow me to have a sight, at least, of my sisters; instead of seeing your own adored body, which you will not allow me to do. These fragrant curls dangling all round your head;

these cheeks as tender and smooth as my own; this delightfully warm bosom; that face of yours that I shall only be able to know anything about by looking at our baby! So please be sweet and humour my craving—and make your Psyche happy, who loves you so much. I no longer feel so anxious to look at you, or so frightened of the darkness of the night, when I have you safe in my arms, light of my life!" Her voice and sweet caresses broke down her husband's resistance. He wiped her eyes dry with his hair, granted what she asked and as usual disappeared again before the day broke.

The two sisters, their plot arranged, landed from their ship and without even visiting their parents, hurried straight to the rock and with extraordinary daring leaped down from it without waiting for the breeze to belly out their robes. However, the West Wind was bound to obey its master's order, reluctant though he might be; he caught them in his robe as they fell and brought them to the ground.

At once they rushed into the palace and embraced their victim with what she took for sisterly affection. Then, with cheerful laughter masking their treachery, they cried: "Why, Psyche, you're not nearly so slim as you used to be. You'll be a mother before very long. We're so delighted you're going to have a baby, and what a joy it'll be for the whole household. Oh, how we shall love to nurse your golden baby for you! If it takes after its parents, as it ought to, it will be a perfect little Cupid."

By this pretended love they gradually wormed themselves into her confidence. Seeing that they were tired because of their journey, she invited them to sit down and rest while water was heated for them; and when they had taken their baths, she gave them spiced sausages and other marvellously tasty dishes, while an unseen harpist played for them at her orders, as well as an unseen flautist, and a choir sang the most ravishing songs. But even such honey-sweet music as that failed to soften the hard hearts of those wicked women. They insidiously brought the conversation round to her husband, asking her who he was and from where his family came.

Psyche was very simple-minded and, forgetting what story she had told them before, invented a new one. She said that he was a middle-aged merchant from the next province, very rich, with slightly grizzled hair. Then breaking the conversation off short, she loaded them with valuable presents and sent them away in their windy carriage.

As they returned home, borne aloft by the peaceful breath of Zephyrus, they held a discussion in these terms: "Now, what do you make of the monstrous lies she tells us? First the silly creature says that her husband is a very young man with a downy beard, and then she says that he's middle-aged with grizzled hair!

Quick work, eh? You may depend upon it that the evil woman is either hiding something from us, or else she never sees what her husband looks like."

"Whatever the truth may be, we must ruin her as soon as possible. But if she really has never seen her husband, then he must be a god, and her baby will be a god too. If that happens, which Heaven forbid, I'll hang myself at once. So now let us return to our parents and start telling some lies to suit our plans."

In this state of excitement, they arrived and gave their father and mother an offhand greeting. Their disturbed feelings kept them awake all night, and in the morning the evil women hurried to the rock and floated down into the valley as usual with the help of the West Wind. Rubbing their eyelids hard until they managed to squeeze out a few tears, they went to Psyche and said: "Oh, sister, ignorance is indeed bliss! There you sit quite happily, without the least suspicion of the terrible danger that threatens you, while we are in absolute anguish about it. You see, we watch over your interests indefatigably and are deeply upset by your misfortunes. For we are reliably informed, and since we share your sorrows and fortunes we have to tell you that the husband who comes secretly gliding into your bed at night is an enormous snake with many twisting coils, its neck bloodily swollen with deadly poison, its jaws gaping wide. Remember what Apollo's oracle said: that you were destined to marry a savage wild beast. Very many of the farmers who go hunting in the woods around this place have met him coming home at nightfall from his feeding ground and have seen him swimming across the river nearby. They all say that he won't pamper you with delicate meals much longer, but that when your nine months are nearly up he will eat you alive, when you have a tenderer morsel inside you. So you had better make up your mind whether you will come away and live with us—we are so eager to look after our beloved sister—or whether you prefer to stay here with this fiendish reptile until you finish up in his guts. Perhaps you're fascinated by living here alone with your voices all day and at night making secret and disgusting love to a poisonous snake. But at all events we have done what we could as dutiful sisters."

Poor silly Psyche was aghast at the dreadful news. She lost all control of herself, trembled, turned deathly pale and, forgetting all the warnings her husband had given her and all her own promises, plunged headlong into the abyss of misfortune. She gasped out brokenly: "Dearest sisters, thank you for being so kind. I do believe that the people who told you this story were not making it up. The fact is I have never seen my husband's face and haven't the least idea where he comes from. I only hear him speaking to me at night in whispers, so that I have to put up with a husband I know nothing about, who evidently hates the light of day. So I have every reason to suppose, as you do, that he must be some animal. Besides, he is always giving me frightful warnings about what will happen if I try to see what he looks like. So please, if you can advise your sister what to do in this dreadful situation, tell me at once; otherwise, all the trouble you have been kind enough to take will be wasted."

The wicked women saw that Psyche's defences were down and her heart laid open to their attacks. They pressed their advantage: "Since we are so closely related," one of them said, "the thought of your danger makes us forget our own. We two have talked the matter over countless times and will show you how to save yourself. This is what you must do. Get hold of a very sharp carving knife, make it sharper still by stropping it on your palm. Then hide it somewhere on your side of the bed. Also, get hold of a lamp. Have it filled full of oil, trim the wick carefully, light it and hide it behind the bedroom tapestry. Do all this with the greatest secrecy and when he visits you as usual, wait until he is stretched out at full length, and you know by his deep breathing that he's fast asleep. Then slip out of bed with the knife in your hand and tiptoe barefooted to the place where you have hidden the lamp. Finally, with its light to assist you, perform your noble deed, plunge the knife down with all your strength at the nape of the serpent's poisonous neck and cut off its head. We promise to help you; the moment you have saved yourself by killing it, we shall come running in and help you to get away at once with all your treasure. After that, we'll marry you to a human being like yourself."

When they saw that Psyche was now determined to follow their suggestion, they went quietly off, terrified to be anywhere near her when the catastrophe came; they were helped up to the rock by the West Wind, ran back to their ships as fast as they could and sailed off at once.

Psyche was left alone, in so far as a woman haunted by hostile Furies can be called alone. Her mind was as restless as a stormy sea. When she first began making preparations for her crime, her resolve was firm; but presently she wavered and started worrying about all the different aspects of her calamity. She hurried, then she dawdled; at one moment she was bold and at another frightened; she felt nervous and then she got angry again. For, although she loathed the animal, she loved the husband it seemed to be. However, as evening drew on, she finally acted rapidly and prepared what was needed to do the dreadful deed.

Night fell, and her husband came to bed, and after preliminary amorous skirmishes he fell fast asleep. Psyche was not naturally either very strong or very brave, but the cruel power of fate made a man of her. Holding the knife in a murderous grip, she uncovered the lamp and let its light shine on the bed.

There lay the gentlest and sweetest of all wild creatures, Cupid himself, lying in all his beauty, and at the sight of him the flame of the lamp spurted joyfully up and the knife turned its edge for shame.

When Psyche saw this wonderful sight she was terrified. She lost all control of her senses and, pale as death, fell trembling to her knees, where she tried to hide the knife by plunging it in her own heart. She would have succeeded, too, had the knife not shrunk from the crime and twisted itself out of her foolhardy hands. Faint and unnerved though she was, she began to feel better as she stared at Cupid's divine beauty: his golden hair, washed in ambrosia and still scented with it, curls straying over white neck and flushed cheeks and falling prettily entangled on either side of his head—hair so bright that it darkened the flame of the lamp. At his shoulders grew soft wings of the purest white and, though they were at rest, the tender down fringing the feathers quivered attractively all the time. The rest of his body was so smooth and beautiful that Venus could never have been ashamed to acknowledge him as her son. At the foot of the bed lay this great god's gracious weapons, his bow, quiver and arrows.

Psyche's curiosity could be satisfied only by a close examination of her husband's weapons. She pulled an arrow out of the quiver and touched the point with the tip of her thumb to try its sharpness; but her hand was trembling and she pressed too hard. The skin was pierced and out came a drop or two of blood. So Psyche accidentally fell in love with Love. Burning with greater passion for Cupid even than before, she flung herself panting upon him, desperate with desire, and smothered him with sensual, open-mouthed kisses; her one fear now being that he would wake too soon.

While she clung to him, utterly bewildered with delight, the lamp which she was still holding, whether from horrid treachery or destructive envy, or because it too longed to touch and kiss such a body, spurted a drop of scalding oil on the god's right shoulder. What a bold and impudent lamp, what a worthless servant of Love—for the first lamp was surely invented by some lover who wished to prolong the pleasures of the night—so to scorch the god of all fire! Cupid sprang up in pain and, seeing that the bonds of faith were shattered and in ruins, spread his wings and flew away from the kisses and embraces of his unhappy wife without a word; but not before Psyche had seized his right leg with both hands and clung to it. She looked very queer, carried up like that through the cloudy sky; but soon her strength failed her and she tumbled down to earth again.

Cupid did not desert her as she lay on the ground, but alighted on the top of a cypress nearby, where he stood reproaching her. "Oh, foolish Psyche, it was for your sake that I disobeyed the orders of my mother, Venus! She told me to inflame you with passion for some utterly worthless man, but I preferred to fly down from Heaven and become your lover myself. I know only too well that I acted thoughtlessly, and Cupid, the famous archer, wounds himself with one of his own arrows and marries a girl who mistakes him for a beast; she tries to chop off his head with a knife and darken the eyes that have loved her so greatly. This was the danger of which I warned you again and again, gently begging you to be on your guard. As for those fine sisters of yours who turned you against me and gave you such damnable advice, I'll very soon be avenged on them. But your punishment will simply be that I'll fly away from you." And when he had uttered those words he soared up into the air and was gone.

Psyche lay motionless on the ground, following her husband with her eyes as far as she could and moaning bitterly. When the beat of his wings had carried him aloft clean out of her sight, she flung herself headlong into a river that flowed close by. But the kindly river, out of respect for the god and fearing for itself since even the waters do not escape his fiery intentions, washed her ashore and laid her on the bank, upon the flowery turf.

Pan, the goat-legged country god, happened to be sitting nearby, caressing the mountain nymph Echo and teaching her to repeat all sorts of pretty songs. A flock of she-goats roamed around, browsing greedily on the grass. The goat-footed god was already aware, somehow or other, of Psyche's misfortune, so he gently beckoned to the desolate girl and did what he could to comfort her. "Pretty dear," he said soothingly. "Though I'm only a shepherd and very much of a countryman, I have picked up a good deal of experience in my long life. So if I am right in my conjecture—or my divination, as sensible people would call it—your unsteady and faltering walk, your pallor, your constant sighs and your sad eyes show that you're very much in love. Listen: make no further attempts at suicide by leaping from a precipice or performing any other fatal action. Stop crying and open your heart to Cupid, the greatest of us gods; he's a thoroughly spoilt young fellow whom you must humour by praying to him only in the gentlest, sweetest language."

It is very lucky to be addressed by Pan, but Psyche made no reply. She merely did a reverence to him as a god and went on. She trudged along the road for a while, until she happened to turn into a lane that led off it. Towards evening it brought her to a city of which she soon found out that the husband of one of her sisters was the king. She announced her arrival at the palace and was at once admitted.

After an exchange of greetings and embraces, the queen asked Psyche why she had come. Psyche answered: "You remember your advice about that knife and the beast who pretended to be my husband, and lay with me, and was going to swallow me up voraciously in my misery? Well, I took it, but no sooner had I shone my lamp on the bed than I saw a marvellous sight: Venus's divine son, Cupid himself, lying there in tranquil sleep. The joy and relief were too great for me. I quite lost my head and didn't know how to satisfy my longing for him; but then, by a dreadful accident, a drop of burning oil from the lamp spurted on to his shoulder. The pain woke him at once. When he saw me holding the lamp and the knife, he shouted: 'How could you do me such a mischief? I divorce you; take your things away. I am going to marry your sister instead.' And he named you. Then he called for the West Wind, who blew me out of the palace and landed me here."

Psyche had hardly finished her story before her sister, madly jealous of her and burning with lust, went to her husband and deceived him with a cunning tale, declaring that she had heard her parents were dead. Off she went and when at last she reached the rock though another wind altogether was blowing, she shouted with misplaced confidence: "Here I come, Cupid, a woman worthy of your love. West Wind, convey your mistress!" Then she took a headlong leap;

but she never reached the valley, either dead or alive, because the rocks cut her to pieces as she fell and scattered her flesh and guts all over the mountainside. So she got what she deserved and died, and the birds and beasts feasted on her remains.

And it was not long before a second vengeance followed. For Psyche wandered on and on until she came to another city, where the other sister lived and took her in by the same deceitful story as she had told to her sister. She, too, was anxious to supplant her sister by making a criminal marriage, hurried to the rock and died in exactly the same way.

III

PSYCHE CONTINUED on her travels through country after country, searching for Cupid; but he was lying in his mother's own room and groaning for pain because of his wound from the lamp. Meanwhile a white gull, of the sort that skims the surface of the sea flapping the waves with its wings, dived down into the water; there it met Venus, who was having a bathe and a swim, and brought her the news that her son Cupid was suffering from a severe and painful burn, from which it was doubtful whether he would recover. It told her, too, that every sort of scandal about Venus's family was going around.

People were saying that Psyche's son had flown down to the mountain to have an affair with a whore, while she herself had gone off to swim in the sea: "The result is, they declare, that Pleasure, Grace and Wit have disappeared from the earth and everything there has become ugly, dull and slovenly. Nobody bothers any longer about his wife, about his friends or his children; everything is in a state of disorder, and weddings are viewed with bitter distaste and regarded as disgusting."

This talkative, meddlesome bird squawked into Venus's ears and succeeded in setting her against her son. She grew very angry and cried: "So my promising lad has taken a mistress, has he? Here, gull—you seem to be the only creature left with any true affection for me—tell me, do you know the name of the creature who has seduced my poor simple boy? Is she one of the Nymphs, or one of the Seasons, or one of the Muses, or one of my own train of Graces?"

The garrulous bird was very ready to talk. "Lady, I cannot say; but if I remember rightly the story is that your son has fallen desperately in love with a human named Psyche."

Venus was absolutely furious. "What! With her, of all women? With Psyche, the usurper of my beauty, the rival of my glory? This is worse and worse. It was through me that he got to know the girl. Does the brat take me for a procuress?"

Thus lamenting, she rose from the sea at once and hurried aloft to her golden room where she found Cupid lying ill, as the gull had told her. As she entered she bawled out at the top of her voice: "Now *is* this decent behaviour? A fine credit you are to our divine family and a fine reputation you're building up for yourself. You trample your mother's orders underfoot as though she had no authority over you whatsoever, and instead of tormenting her enemy with a dishonourable passion, as you were ordered to do, you have the impudence to sleep with the girl yourself, at your age! To have someone I hate as my daughter-in-law! And I suppose you also think, you worthless, debauched, revolting boy, that you're the only child I'm going to have and that I'm past the age of child-bearing! Please understand that I'm quite capable of having another son, if I please, and a far better one than you. However, to make you feel the disgrace still more keenly, I think I'll legally adopt one of my slaves and hand over to him your wings, torch, bow and arrows, which you have been using in ways for which I never intended them. And I have every right to do that, because not one of them was supplied by your father. The fact is that you have been mischievous from your earliest years and always delighted in hurting people. You have often had the bad manners to shoot at your elders, and as for me, your mother, you rob me day after day, you matricidal wretch, and have constantly stuck me full of your arrows. You sneer at me and call me 'the widow', and show not the slightest respect for your brave, invincible stepfather; in fact, you do your best to annoy me by setting him after other women and making me jealous. But you'll soon be sorry that you played all those tricks; I warn you that this marriage of yours is going to leave a sour, bitter taste in your mouth."

Then, to herself: "Everyone is laughing at me and I
haven't the faintest idea what to do or where to go.
How in the world am I to catch and cage the little
viper? I suppose I'd better go for help to old Sobriety
to whom I've always been so dreadfully rude for the
sake of this spoilt son of mine. Must I really have anything to do with that dowdy, countrified woman? Well,
revenge is sweet from whatever quarter it comes. Yes,
I fear that she's the only person who can do anything
for me. She'll give the little beast a thrashing; confiscate
his quiver, blunt his arrows, tear the string off his bow
and quench his torch. Worse than that, she'll shave off
his hair, which I have often bound up with my own
hands so that it glittered with gold, and clip those lovely wings of his which I once whitened with the dazzling
milk of my own breast. When that's been done, I'll feel
I've got my own back for the harm he's done me."

After this declaration she rushed out of doors in a
furious rage truly worthy of Venus and at once ran
into Ceres and Juno, who noticed how angry she
looked and asked her why she was spoiling the beauty
of her bright eyes with so sullen a frown. "Thank goodness I met you," she answered, "I needed you to calm
me down. There is something you can do for me, if
you'll be kind enough. Please make careful inquiries
for the whereabouts of a runaway vagabond called
Psyche—I'm sure you must have heard all about her

216

and the family scandal she's caused by her affair with ... my unmentionable son."

Of course they knew all about it, and tried to soothe her fury. "Lady," they said, "what terrible sin has he committed? Why try to thwart his pleasures and kill the girl with whom he's fallen in love? It is no crime, surely, to beam amiably at a pretty girl? You imagine that he's still only a boy because he carries his years so gracefully, but you simply must realize that he's a young man now. Have you forgotten his age? A mother and a woman of the world, ought you to persist in poking your nose into your son's pleasures and blame the handsome boy for those very sensual talents and erotic inclinations that he inherits directly from yourself? What god or man will have any patience with you, when you go about all the time waking sexual desire in people but at the same time try to repress similar feelings in your own son? Is it really your intention to close down the factory of woman's universal weakness?

The goddesses, in thus fulsomely defending Cupid, showed their fear of his arrows, even when he was not about. Venus, seeing that they refused to take a serious view of her wrongs, indignantly turned her back on them and hurried off again to the sea.

Meanwhile, Psyche was restlessly wandering about day and night in search of her husband. However angry he might be, she hoped to make him relent either by coaxing him with wifely endearments or abasing herself in abject repentance. One day she noticed a temple on the top of a steep hill. She said to herself: "I wonder if my husband is there?" so she walked quickly towards the hill, her heart full of love and hope, and reached the temple with some difficulty, after climbing ridge after ridge. But when she arrived at the sacred couch she found it heaped with votive gifts of wheatsheaves, wheat chaplets and ears of barley, also sickles and other harvest implements, but all scattered about untidily, as though flung down on a hot summer day by careless reapers.

She began to sort all these things carefully, and arrange them in their proper places, feeling that she must behave respectfully towards every deity whose temple she happened to visit and implore the compassionate help of the whole heavenly family. The temple belonged to the generous Goddess Ceres, who found her busily and energetically at work and at once called out from afar: "Oh, you poor Psyche! Venus is furious and searching everywhere for you. She wants to be cruelly revenged and to punish you with all the strength of her divine power. I am surprised that you can spare the time to look after my affairs for me, or think of anything at all but your own safety."

Psyche's hair streamed across the temple floor as she prostrated herself at Ceres's feet, which she wetted with

218

her tears. She implored her protection: "I beseech you, Goddess—by your fruitful right hand, by the happy ceremony of harvest-home, by the secret contents of your baskets, by the winged dragons of your chariot, by the furrows of Sicily from which a cruel god once ravished your daughter Proserpine, by the wheels of his chariot, by the earth that closed upon her, by her dark descent and gloomy wedding, by her happy torch-lit return to earth, and by the other mysteries which Eleusis, your Attic sanctuary, silently conceals—help me: oh, please, help your unhappy suppliant Psyche. Allow me, just for a few days, to hide myself under that stack of wheatsheaves, until the great goddess's rage has had time to cool down; or until I have somewhat recovered from my long and tiring troubles."

Ceres answered: "Your tears and prayers go straight to my heart, and I would dearly love to help you; but I can't afford to offend my relative. She has been one of my best friends for ages and ages and really has a very good heart. You'd better leave this temple at once and think yourself lucky that I don't have you placed under arrest."

Psyche went away, twice as sad as she had come: she had never expected such a rebuff. But soon she saw below her in the valley another beautifully constructed temple in the middle of a dark sacred grove. She feared to miss any chance, even a remote one, of putting things right for herself, so she went down to

implore the protection of the deity of the place, whoever it might be. She saw various splendid offerings hanging from branches of the grove and from the temple
door-posts; among them were garments embroidered
with gold letters that spelt out the name of the goddess
to whom all were dedicated, namely Juno, and record-
ed the favours which she had granted their donors.

Psyche fell on her knees, wiped away her tears and,
embracing the temple altar, still warm from a recent
sacrifice, began to pray. "Sister and wife of great
Jupiter! You may be residing in one of your ancient
temples on Samos—the Samians boast that you were
born on their island and uttered your infant cries
there, and they brought you up. Or you may be visiting your happy city of Carthage on its high hill, where
you are adored as a virgin travelling across Heaven in
a lion-drawn chariot. Or you may be watching over
the famous walls of Argos, past which the river
Inachus flows, where you are adored as the Queen of
Heaven, the Thunderer's bride. Wherever you are,
you whom the whole East venerates as Zygia the
Goddess of Marriage, and the whole West as Lucina,
Goddess of Childbirth, I appeal to you now as Juno
the Protectress. I beg you to watch over me in my
overwhelming misfortune and rescue me from the
dangers that threaten me. You see, Goddess, I am very
tired and very frightened, and I know that you're

always ready to help women who are about to have babies, if they get into any sort of trouble."

Hearing Psyche's appeal, Juno appeared in all her august glory and said: "I should be only too pleased to help you, but I can't possibly go against the wishes of my daughter-in-law Venus, whom I have always loved as though she were my own child. Besides, I am forbidden by the laws to harbour any fugitive slave-girl without her owner's consent."

Psyche was distressed by this second shipwreck of her hopes and felt quite unable to go on looking for her winged husband. She gave up all hope of safety and said to herself: "Where can I turn for help, now that even these powerful goddesses will do nothing for me but express their sympathy? Tangled as I am in all these snares, where can I go? Where is there a building, or any dark place, in which I can hide myself from the inescapable eyes of great Venus? The fact is, my dear Psyche, that you must borrow a little male courage, you must boldly renounce all idle hopes and make a voluntary surrender to your mistress. Late though it is, you must at least try to calm her rage by submissive behaviour. Besides, after this long search, you have quite a good chance of finding your husband at his mother's house."

Psyche's decision to undertake this appeal was risky and even suicidal, but she prepared herself for it by considering what sort of appeal she ought to make to the goddess.

Venus meanwhile gave up employing earthly means to find Psyche and returned to Heaven, where she ordered her chariot to be got ready. The fact that it had lost some of its gold—chiselled away to make a filigree decoration—make it more valuable, not less. It had been her husband the goldsmith Vulcan's wedding present to her. Four white doves from the flock in constant attendance on her, flew happily forward and offered their rainbow-coloured necks to the jewelled harness and, when Venus mounted, drew the chariot along with enthusiasm. Behind, played a crowd of naughty sparrows and other little birds that sang very sweetly in announcement of the goddess's arrival.

Now the clouds vanished, the sky opened and the high upper air received her joyfully. Her singing retinue were not in the least afraid of swooping eagles or greedy hawks, and she drove straight to the royal citadel of Jupiter, where she demanded the immediate services of Mercury, the Town-crier of Heaven, in a matter of great urgency. When Jupiter nodded his sapphire brow in assent, Venus was delighted; she retired from Heaven and gave Mercury, who was now accompanying her, careful instructions. "Brother from Arcadia, you know that I, your sister, have never in my life undertaken any business at all without your assistance, and you know how long I have been unable to find my slave-girl who is in hiding. So the only solution is for you to make a public announcement offering a reward to the person who finds her. My orders must be carried out immediately. Her person must be accurately described so that nobody will be able to plead ignorance as an excuse for harbouring her."

And as she spoke she handed him a document indicating Psyche's name and other particulars and immediately went home. Mercury did as he was told. He went from country to country crying out everywhere: "If any person can apprehend and seize the person of a king's runaway daughter, Venus's slave-girl, by name Psyche, or give any information that will lead to her discovery, let such a person go to Mercury, Town-crier of Heaven, in his temple behind the Circus column beside the temple of Murcia in Rome. The reward offered is as follows: seven sweet kisses from the mouth of the said Venus herself and one delicious thrust of her honeyed tongue between his lips."

A jealous competitive spirit naturally fired all mankind when they heard this reward announced, and it was this that, most of all, put an end to Psyche's hesitation. She was already near her mistress's gate when she was met by one of the household, named Habit, who screamed out at once at the top of her voice: "You wicked slave-girl, you! So you've discovered at last that you have a mistress, eh? But don't pretend, you brazen-faced thing, that you haven't heard of the huge trouble that you've caused us in our search for you. Well, I'm glad that you've fallen into my hands, because you're safe here—safe inside the doors of Hell, and there won't be any delay in your punishment either, you obstinate creature." She seized Psyche's hair violently and dragged her into Venus's presence, though she came along willingly enough.

When Venus saw her brought into her presence she burst into the hilarious laugh of a woman who is desperately angry. She shook her head and scratched her right ear. "So you condescend," she cried, "to pay your respects to your mother-in-law? Or perhaps you have come to visit your husband, hearing that he's dangerously ill from the burn you gave him? I promise you the sort of welcome that a good mother-in-law is bound to give her son's wife." She clapped her hands for her slaves, Anxiety and Grief, and when they ran up, gave Psyche over to them for punishment. Obeying their mistress's orders, they flogged her cruelly and tortured her in other ways besides, after which they brought her back to Venus's presence.

Once more Venus yelled with laughter: "Just look at her!" she cried. "Look at the whore! That big belly of hers makes me feel quite sorry for her. By Heaven, it wrings my grandmotherly heart! How wonderful to be called a grandmother at my time of life! And to think that the son of this disgusting slave will be called Venus's own grandchild! No, but of course that is nonsense. A marriage between unequal partners, celebrated in the depth of the country without witnesses and lacking even the consent of the bride's father, can't possibly be recognized by law; your child will be a bastard, even if I permit you to bring it into the world."

With this, she flew at poor Psyche, tore her clothes to shreds, pulled out handfuls of her hair, then grabbed her by the shoulders and gave her head a violent shaking. Next she took wheat, barley, millet, lentils, beans and the seeds of poppy and vetch, and mixed them all together into a heap. "You look such a dreadful sight, slave," she said, "that the only way that you are ever likely to get a lover is by hard work, so now I'll test you myself, to find out what you can do. Do you see this pile of seeds all mixed together? Sort out the different kinds, stack them in separate heaps and do the job to my satisfaction before nightfall." When she had given this great heap of seeds to Psyche to deal with, she flew off to attend some wedding feast or other.

Psyche made no attempt to set about the inextricable mass but sat gazing dumbly at it, until a very small ant, one of the country sort, realized the stupendous nature of her task. Pity for Psyche as wife of the mighty God of Love set it cursing the cruelty of her mother-in-law and scurrying about to round up every ant in the district. "Take pity," she said, "on this pretty girl, you busy children of the generous Earth. She's the wife of Love himself and her life is in great danger. Quick, quick, to the rescue!"

They came rushing up as fast as their six legs would carry them, wave upon wave of ants, and began working furiously to sort the pile out, grain by grain. Soon they had arranged it all tidily in separate heaps and had run off again at once.

Venus returned that evening, a little drunk, smelling of fragrant ointments and swathed in rose-wreaths. When she saw with what prodigious speed Psyche had finished the task, she said: "You didn't do a hand's stroke yourself, you wicked thing. This is the work of someone whom you have made infatuated with you—though you'll be sorry for it." She threw her part of a coarse loaf and went to bed.

Meanwhile she had confined Cupid to an isolated room in the depths of the house, partly to prevent him from playing his usual naughty tricks and so making his injury worse; partly to keep him away from his sweetheart. So the lovers spent a miserable night, unable to visit each other, although under the same roof.

As soon as the Goddess of Dawn had set her team moving across the sky, Venus called Psyche and said:

"Do you see the grove fringing the bank of that stream over there, with fruit bushes hanging low over the water? Shining golden sheep are wandering about in it, without a shepherd to look after them. I want you to go there and by some means or other fetch me a hank of their precious wool."

Psyche rose willingly enough, but with no intention of obeying Venus's orders; she had made up her mind to throw herself in the stream and so end her sorrows. But a green reed, producer of sweet music, was blown upon by some divine breeze and uttered words of wisdom: "I know, Psyche, what dreadful sorrows you have suffered, but you must not pollute these sacred waters by a suicide. And, another thing, you must not go into the grove, to risk your life among those dangerous sheep, until the heat of the sun is past. It so infuriates the beasts that they kill any human being who ventures among them. Either they gore them with sharp horns, or butt them to death with their stony foreheads, or bite them with their poisonous teeth. Wait until the afternoon wears to a close and the serene whispers of these waters lull them asleep. Hide meanwhile under that tall plane-tree which drinks the same water as I do, and as soon as the sheep calm down, go into the grove nearby and gather the wisps of golden wool that you'll find sticking on every briar there."

It was a simple, kindly reed, telling Psyche how to save herself, and she took its advice, which proved to be sound: that evening she was able to return to Venus with a whole lapful of the delicate golden wool. Yet even her performance of this second dangerous task did not satisfy the goddess, who frowned and told her with a cruel smile: "Someone has been helping you again, that's quite clear. But now I'll put your lofty courage and singular prudence to a still severer test. Do you see the summit of that high mountain over there? You'll find that a dark-coloured stream cascades down its precipitous sides into a gorge below and then floods the Stygian marshes and feeds the hoarse River of Cocytus. Here is a little jar. Go off at once and bring it back to me brimful of ice-cold water fetched from the very middle of the stream at the point where it bursts out of the rock."

She gave Psyche a jar of polished crystal and packed her off with renewed and even more menacing threats.

Psyche started at once for the top of the mountain, thinking that there at least she would find a means of ending her wretched life. As she came up to the ridge of the hill she saw what a stupendously dangerous and difficult task had been set her. The dreadful waters of the river burst out from halfway up an enormously tall, steep, slippery precipice; cascaded down into a narrow conduit, which they had hollowed for themselves, and flowed unseen into the gorge below. On both sides of their outlet she saw fierce dragons crawling, never asleep, always on guard with unwinking eyes and stretching their long necks over the water. And the waters themselves seemed to have voices, which called out: "Be off! What are you doing? Take care! What are you at? Look out! Off with you! You'll die!"

Psyche stood still as stone; the utter impossibility of her task was so overwhelming that she could no longer even relieve herself by tears—that last comfort. But the kind, sharp eyes of good Providence noticed when her innocent soul was in trouble, and Jupiter's royal bird, the rapacious eagle, suddenly sailed down to her with outstretched wings. He gratefully remembered the ancient debt that he owed to Cupid for having helped him to carry the Phrygian cup-bearer to Jupiter, and so, flying past Psyche's face, addressed her with these words: "Silly, inexperienced Psyche, how can you ever hope to steal one drop of this most sacred and terrifying stream? Surely you have heard that Jupiter himself fears the waters of Styx, and that just as human beings swear by the Blessed Gods, so they swear by the Sovereign Styx. But let me take that little jar." He quickly snatched it from her grasp and soared off on his strong wings, steering a zigzag course between the two rows of furious fangs and vibrating three-forked tongues. The stream was reluctant to give up its water and warned him to escape while he still could, but he explained that the Goddess Venus wanted the water and pretended that she had commissioned him to fetch it; a story which carried some weight with the stream. Psyche, accepting the brimful jar with delight, quickly returned with it to Venus, but still could not appease her fury. Instead, threatening even worse and grimmer acts of villainy, she said with a smile which seemed to spell the girl's ruin: "You must be a witch, a very clever, very wicked witch, else you could never have carried out my orders so diligently, but I have still one more task for you to perform, my dear girl. Take this box (and she gave it to her) and go down to the Underworld to the death-palace of Orcus. Hand it to Proserpine and ask her to send this box back to me with a little of her beauty in it, enough to last for at least one short day. Tell her that I have had to make such a drain on my own store, as a result of looking after my sick son, that I have none left. Then come back with the box at once, because I must rub its contents over me before I go to the theatre of the gods tonight."

This seemed to Psyche the end of everything, since her orders were to go down to the Underworld of Tartarus. Psyche saw that she was undisguisedly being sent to her immediate death. She went at once to a high tower, deciding that her straightest and easiest way to the Underworld was to throw herself down from it. But the tower suddenly broke into human speech: "Poor child," it said, "do you really mean to commit suicide by jumping down from me? How rash of you to lose hope just before the end of your trials. Don't you realize that as soon as the breath is out of your body you will indeed go right to the depths of Tartarus, but that once you take that way there's no hope of return? Listen to me. The famous Greek city of Lacedaemon is not far from here. Go there at once and ask to be directed to Taenarus, which is rather an out of the way place to find. Once you get there you'll find one of the ventilation holes of Dis. Open gates lead on to a pathless way which, once you have started along it, leads directly to the palace of Orcus. But take care not to go empty-handed through that place of darkness; carry with you two pieces of barley bread soaked in honey water, one in each hand, and two coins in your mouth.

"When you have gone a good way along that deadly road you'll meet a lame ass loaded with wood, and its lame driver will ask you to hand him some sticks which the ass has dropped. Pass him by in silence. Then you will soon reach the river of the dead, where the ferryman Charon will at once demand his fee before he takes you across in his patched boat among the crowds of ghosts. It seems that avarice flourishes even among the dead, because Charon, the tax-gatherer of Pluto, does not do anything for nothing. (A poor man on

CUPID AND PSYCHE

the point of death is expected to have his passage-fee ready; but if he can't get hold of a coin, he isn't allowed to die.) Anyhow, give the filthy old man one of your coins, but let him take it from your mouth, with his own hand. While you are being ferried across the sluggish stream, the corpse of an old man will float by; he will raise a putrid hand and beg you to haul him into the boat. But you must be careful not to yield to any feeling of pity for him; that is forbidden. Once ashore, you will meet three old women some distance away from the bank. They will be weaving cloth and will ask you to help them. To touch the cloth is also forbidden. All these apparitions, and others like them, are snares set for you by Venus; her object is to make you let go one of the sops you are carrying, and you must understand that the loss of even one of them would be fatal—it would prevent your return to this world. They are for you to give to the huge, fierce, formidable hound with three massive heads, whose thunderous barking assails the dead; though they have no need to be frightened by him because he can do them no harm.

"He keeps perpetual guard at the threshold of Proserpine's dark palace, the desolate abode of Pluto. Muzzle him with one of your sops and you'll find it easy to get past him into the presence of Proserpine herself. She'll give you a warm welcome, offer you a comfortable seat and have you brought a magnificent

232

meal. But sit on the ground, ask for a piece of common bread and eat nothing else. Then deliver your message, and she'll give you what you came for.

"As you go out, throw the dog the remaining sop to appease his savagery, then pay the greedy ferryman the remaining coin and, after crossing his river, go back by the way you came until you see once again the familiar constellations of Heaven. One last, important warning: be careful not to open or even look at the box you carry back; that hidden receptacle of divine beauty is not for you to explore."

Such were the terms in which the prophetic tower offered its predictions. Psyche went at once to Taenarus where, armed with the coins and the two sops, she ran down the road to the Underworld. She passed in silence by the lame man with the ass, paid Charon the first coin, stopped her ears to the entreaties of the floating corpse, refused to be taken in by the appeal of the spinning women, pacified the dreadful dog with the first sop and entered Proserpine's palace. There she refused the comfortable chair and the tempting meal, sat humbly at Proserpine's feet, content with a crust of common bread, and finally delivered Venus's message. Psyche filled the box with the secret substance and went away; then she stopped the dog's barking with the second sop, paid Charon with the second coin and returned from the Underworld, feeling in far better health and spirits than while on her way down there and delighted to see the bright daylight again. Though she was in a hurry to complete her errand she allowed her curiosity to get the better of her. She said to herself; "I should be a fool to carry this divine beauty without borrowing a tiny touch of it for my own use: I must do everything possible to please my beautiful lover."

Amid these reflections, she opened the box, but it contained no beauty nor anything else, so far as she saw; instead out crept a truly Stygian and deadly sleep which, as soon as the cover was taken off, immediately seized her and wrapped her in a dense cloud of drowsiness. She fell prostrate and lay there like a corpse, on the path, just where she had been standing.

Cupid, now recovered from his injury and unable to bear Psyche's long absence a moment longer, flew out through the lofty window of the bedroom where he had been held prisoner. His wings invigorated by their long rest, he hurried to Psyche, carefully brushed away the cloud of sleep from her body and shut it up again in its box, then roused her with a harmless prick of an arrow. "Poor girl," he said, "your curiosity has once more nearly ruined you. Hurry now and complete the task which my mother set you; and I'll see to everything else." With these words he flew off, and she sprang up at once to deliver Proserpine's present.

But Cupid, who had fallen more deeply in love with Psyche than ever and was alarmed by his mother's sudden respectability, returned to his old tricks. He flew at great speed to the very highest Heaven and flung himself as a suppliant at Jupiter's feet, where he pleaded his case. Jupiter pinched his cheeks and kissed his hand. Then he said: "My masterful child, you never pay me the respect which has been decreed me by the Council of Gods, and you're always shooting your arrows into my heart—the very seat of the laws that govern the elements and the constellations of the sky. Often you defile it with mortal love affairs, contrary to the laws, notably the Julian edict, and the public peace, injuring my reputation and authority by involving me in sordid love intrigues and disagreeably transforming my serene appearance into that of serpent, fire, wild beast, bird or bull. Nevertheless, I can't forget how often I've nursed you on my knees and how soft-hearted I can be, so I'll do whatever you ask. But please realize that you must protect yourself against envious persons, and if any other girl of really outstanding beauty happens to be about on the earth today, remember the good turn I am doing you and get her to recompense me for it."

After saying these words, he ordered Mercury to call a council of all the gods, with a penalty of ten thousand *sestertii* for non-appearance. Everyone was afraid to be fined such a sum, so the Celestial Theatre filled up at once, and Almighty Jupiter from his sublime throne read the following address:

"Right honourable gods and goddesses whose names are registered in the White Roll of the Muses, you all know the young man over there whom I have brought up from boyhood and to whose youthfully passionate nature I have thought it advisable to administer certain curbs. It is enough to remind you of the daily complaints that come in of his adulterous living and practising of every sort of vice. Well, we must stop the young rascal from doing anything of the sort again by fastening the fetters of marriage securely upon him. He has found and seduced a girl called Psyche, and so let him have her, hold her, possess her and enjoy her embraces from this time forth and for evermore."

Then he turned to Venus: "My daughter, you have no occasion to be sad or ashamed that your rank and station in Heaven has been disgraced by your son's mortal match; for I'll see that the marriage is one between social equals, legitimate and in accordance with civil law." He ordered Mercury to fetch Psyche at once and escort her up to Heaven. When she arrived he took a cup of ambrosia and handed it to her.

"Drink, Psyche, and become an immortal," he said. "Cupid will now never fly away from your arms, but will remain your husband for ever."

Presently a great wedding feast was prepared. Cupid reclined in the place of honour with Psyche's head resting on his breast; Jupiter was placed next, with Juno and then all the other gods and goddesses in order. Jupiter was served with nectar, the wine of the gods, by the rustic boy, his personal cup-bearer; Bacchus attended to everyone else. Vulcan was the chef; the Seasons decorated the palace with red roses and other flowers, the Graces sprinkled balsam water; the Muses chanted harmoniously; Apollo sang to his own lyre; and fair Venus came forward and performed a fine step-dance in time to the music, while Satyrus and Paniscus played on their pipes. And so Psyche was married to Cupid and in due time she bore him her child, a daughter whose name was Pleasure.

That was the story the witless and drunken old woman told to the girl prisoners, and, standing not far off, regretted that I had no pen or tablets to commit such a fine tale to writing.